Deadly Autumn Harvest

Deadly Autumn Harvest is first published in English
the United Kingdom in 2023 by Corylus Books Ltd,
and was originally published in Romanian as
Toamna se numara cadavrele in 2020.

Corylus Books Ltd

corylusbooks.com

ISBN 978-1-7392989-1-3

Deadly Autumn Harvest

Tony Mott

Translated by Marina Sofia

Published by Corylus Books Ltd

1

The First

The moon was as thin as an arched pine-needle. When you looked at it through SkyView, it still appeared full, and the stars were definitely still there even if you couldn't see them with the naked eye. You could see the stars on your phone even through the clouds, even through walls. But there were no clouds tonight.

The woman pointed her phone towards the forest and looked at the constellation of Leo. She loved that one: on her screen it appeared to be a majestic lion. She had downloaded the app back in August, when there'd been a meteor shower but she had hardly been able to spot anything in the sky. So she had watched the stars shooting across her screen instead. She thought it was close enough to the real thing to make a wish. She wished for a child, and if it were a boy, she would name him Rasalas, after one of the stars of the constellation of Leo. Since then, she had looked at the sky every evening. She knew how important it was to manifest your wish by believing in it fervently, as if she already had the child.

She hiccupped. Somebody somewhere must be talking about her.

The street was deserted, she could see the Șchei Gate at the far end. She took the path above the stadium and then onto Lacea Street. The Heroes' Cemetery was barely lit, maybe they should put some lamps on the tombstones. St Paraschiva Church was on the right, bathed in a warm glow, but the graveyard was dark. She had often passed here before and had never heard or seen anything out of order.

The wind carried the sound of footsteps towards her, the footsteps of a man walking behind her, the sound heightened by the echo. She was sure it was a man from the way he walked.

He watched her hair shining, coming alive each time she passed under a streetlight. A mane of blonde, curly hair turning into a halo, then dimming, then reappearing under the next light. He followed her all the way home.

When she stopped, he hid behind a car. She turned her head but could see nothing. She hesitated, as if caught up in some game.

Why could she not remember to put the keys in the zippered pocket in her handbag? She searched again. She leant her left shoulder against the gate and used both hands to rifle through her bag. She found her phone and dropped it back in. Then it occurred to her that she should have used it to shine a light into her handbag and help her search.

The sudden silence told her that something had changed. There was no sound of footsteps anymore. A light breeze lifted up the hem of her dress, and the air was colder. The trees in the forest above her rustled, and she felt a shiver pass through her body. She tried to turn, but the man grabbed her waist with one hand, pulled her towards him, then covered her face with a fetid rag. She tried to scream, but the cloth filled her mouth and the sounds around her became fainter and fainter. She felt a hand on her neck, struggled to free herself. She heard the clink of the keys in the man's hands. Her throat seemed freer now. She thought she was about to fall, but once they entered the garden, she felt light. Floating, almost dancing, though no music could be heard.

It was so dark you couldn't see a single star.

2

The cold is a dead man's best friend. Low temperatures help preserve the body. She had learnt to befriend dead bodies a long time ago, but she still had a difficult relationship with the cold. Probably because she was still alive.

Those were the kind of jokes Gigi liked to crack every now and then, to scare the people around her. She would be the one laughing the loudest of all, throwing back her head, shaking her curly blonde mane while roaring with laughter.

So a holiday in Greece at the end of August should have been perfect for her. A two-week holiday was a luxury that she hadn't allowed herself for many years – possibly never, but Radu had insisted and she had given in. Actually, Radu had arranged everything: he had rented a villa in Halkidiki, hadn't given her a chance to protest, they got into the car and drove for fourteen hours, while she mostly dozed in the passenger seat. She had worried about leaving her rebellious black cat Morty on his own, Radu's brother Raul had solemnly promised he would visit daily to feed him and even bring his daughters over to play with him.

She was still not entirely sure how she felt about Radu moving in with her. They had got together when she broke up with Vlad. That relationship had been utterly impossible, and neither of them had emerged from it unscathed. Vlad was not just her partner in crime, as she liked to joke, but also the chief of police, while she was still comparatively new to the investigation side of things. His support had been crucial to her, and she had started mixing up professional and personal interest, and fallen for him in such a big way that she had set aside the fact that he was married, as if it were a mere detail that could be resolved somehow. When the relationship with Vlad became a battlefield, she had turned to Radu.

The city was still asleep. Republicii Street was completely empty, aside from two street cleaners, a young man and a young woman in hi-viz vests, scrabbling around in a rubbish bin, to empty it without lifting the plastic bag. Even the pretzel place – the one with the long queues – was still shut at this time.

Gigi was wearing trainers; her steps could not be heard at all. She would have liked to be invisible. She always preferred the streets when there were few people around, but she knew she had at most another hour to go before all the tourists would be out like termites. Of course she realised that tourists were essential to the lifeblood of the city, that it helped local businesses, but she hated them, the way they attacked everything and swarmed all over the place in Sfatului Square, nursing a juice all day at one of the outdoor cafés. She seldom went there if she could help it – and it wasn't just because of the tourists. She generally didn't like crowds, the noise, the incessant chatter. In her childhood, she'd had a recurring dream – that everyone had turned to stone and she was the only one awake and alive. Like the prince coming to rescue Sleeping Beauty.

She entered the building of the County Service for Forensic Medicine. She preferred to call it an institute, but Braşov was a little behind the times and still called it a 'service'. She smiled at Nea Pavel, who was reading the newspaper at his desk in the waiting room.

'Good morning, Nea Pavel! Let me give you a hug.'

He stood up, beaming. 'My dearest girl, you're so

radiant, you've got gold dust in your hair!'

Gigi did a pirouette, then went and kissed him on both cheeks.

'Nea Pavel, I think I missed you.'

'Well, I am sure I missed you!'

Nea Pavel was her best friend at work. He was the facilities manager and driver. Wise and gentle, he always did his best to look after her, bringing her a cake every now and then despite his wife's misgivings, who preferred keeping things for the family.

'Her Indoors has made some zacuscă, so I brought you three jars. Don't forget them when you leave today, I'll try to remind you.'

'You're so kind, Nea Pavel! Did she scold you again?'

'No, I told her from the start that I would take some for you. But she will make another batch soon, this time mainly red peppers, which I know you like best. She even said she would make some especially for you, but for that you'll have to pay us a visit, otherwise she won't feel like you are being grateful enough.'

'That would be great! The zacuscă, I mean. I'm not so sure about the visit.' Gigi leant towards him confidentially, 'But tell me what's the gossip? Are people still cross with Lemnaru?'

The new director had been brought in less than two months ago, a transfer from Cluj, after many fruitless internal struggles. The older staff had set aside their differences to unite in their hatred of the 'intruder'.

'I think they've started to realise that it's better to stay on his good side. The older people – well, they are younger than me, but you know what I mean – moan a bit every now and then, but they know there's not much they can do. For you and Emil it was easier, but even Mr Ispas has got used to it. The others will need a little more time.'

'What fun. Has Lemnaru not got bored of organising weekly meetings?'

'Not at all. He's so attached to the idea that he will soon call me in to those meetings too.'

'You should come, Nea Pavel.'

He laughed, then put his hand up to cover his mouth.

'Ah, so you still haven't been to the dentist?'

'Not planning to go.'

'But an implant isn't such a big deal.'

'Leave me alone, or no more zacuscă for you!'

It was comforting to be back home. Home for her was her workplace, not the house she had grown up in and where she still lived. Admittedly, it had started to feel less full of dark memories since Radu moved in. She hadn't changed an awful lot, other than buying two bedside table lamps, but she had considered changing the furniture. There might not be any need for that, since Radu was thinking of moving outside the city. Which was probably not a bad idea. He dreamt of a little place in the country, quite isolated, with lots of animals, a mini-zoo, with the animals free to roam. Greece had offered them a model: at their holiday villa, they had a deer, three rabbits destroying the garden, two dogs and countless cats. The house was right on the beach, with a terrace overlooking the sea. That was all she had needed: sleep, sun, reading. Sometimes, dreams come true. She had fallen into a reverie, but Nea Pavel brought her back to reality:

'Emil asked me to tell you that you should read the message he left you.'

'He didn't send me any emails, I checked yesterday.'

'Is that how you spend your weekends?'

'I got back on Friday night, and slept all of Saturday, I was so tired from the journey. But I had time yesterday. Radu has gone to Holland for a week.'

'He said he left it in your folder.'

'I'll check, thanks. Have a good day!'

'You too, and let's hope it's a quiet one.'

The hallway was deserted. A lot of people were still on

holiday. She went to the locker and took off her flowery skirt and fuchsia top, putting on her trousers and jacket instead, both of them white. She liked to wear bright colours outside, but here at work everything was white, not that it was compulsory. She admired colleagues who had turquoise, green or red scrubs, but she preferred to make a clear distinction between the inside and the outside world. White used to the be colour of mourning for medieval queens, and her full name, Regina, a name she hated, must nevertheless have influenced this habit. She checked her clothes again, all impeccable, and tied back her hair.

She passed the director's office. Dr Lemnaru had made a good impression on her, no matter what the others thought. He was a true professional. He had moved to Braşov at the age of nearly sixty not only as a promotion, but also to escape from home, as he liked to joke. But everyone knew that it wasn't really a joke.

He simply let her be, because her status was somewhat special. They had founded a Behavioural Analysis Unit in Braşov last year, with much fanfare, with Dr Regina Alexa as the sole collaborator, but nothing much had happened since. After the Fora case, nothing of interest had turned up. The theory was that they would consult her when they had complicated local cases, but most murders were very mundane.

It was quiet in the office. There were a few files in the in-tray and a handwritten letter in the red folder, probably from Emil. He knew how to turn on the charm.

Dear Gigi,

I hope you had a good holiday, I tried not to bother you with anything while you were away. You can pay me back now. I wanted to spare you, but I couldn't find another solution. You will need to go in my place to the conference on Monday. I'm glad I'm not there to see your face when you find out.

All the documents are online. The presentation, the handouts, the comments. It's the case from last summer, if you remember, when we discovered a single kidney at the autopsy.

Don't fight with Lemnaru, it was his idea to go to this nephrology conference. (Although you might need to go home and get changed, I bet you are dressed inappropriately as usual.)

Glad I could be the target of your swearing today, especially since I'm not around. I love you too. Good luck at the conference.

Emil

She opened the presentation and reminded herself of the case. It was a fairly dull case for a conference, so she thought she might try to see if she could persuade her boss to give it a miss.

She knocked twice on Dr Lemnaru's door and went in.

'Good morning, sir.'

'Good morning Gigi, welcome back! How was your holiday?'

'Warm and pleasant. It did me a world of good.'

'Back with renewed energy. Did Emil tell you about the conference?'

'Yes, he left me everything, including the presentation.'

'So you're going?'

'Do I have a choice?'

'Not at all, don't even try!' Lemnaru smiled.

'But, if you don't mind my asking, what are we doing there? It's not even an interesting case. I assume you know which one I mean.'

'Yes, I know, but we need to build our reputation. We want to be consulted.'

'Consulted?' Gigi stared at him in surprise.

'Yes, I think we should be brought in more frequently for medical emergencies.'

'You mean for diagnosing living people?'

'Yes, our knowledge makes us quite valuable.'

'Possibly, but it's not common practice.'

'The whole world is moving that way though. We examine the connections between various pathologies on dead bodies, so we could be of help.'

'I see. You do know that I'm planning to do my Ph.D. in the Netherlands on forensic psychology and victimology?'

'Yes, you mentioned it. What's the connection?'

'Just that I am more involved in the causes and contexts of those committing crimes. Theoretically at least, I am collaborating with the Police Unit for Behavioural Analysis.'

'I know, Gigi, it all sounds rather grand. But you and I both know how rare those cases are that require your special expertise – or the expertise you will acquire after further studies. I suggest you get involved in what we need right now. There hasn't been a juicy murder in Braşov for ages, if you'll pardon my language, so you intend to specialise in something that we don't have an urgent need for.'

'Maybe not here. But I might become useful at the national level.'

'Aren't you a trifle over-optimistic? Not to mention, rather full of yourself?'

'I didn't mean it to sound like that. But I do think we Romanians need to get better at this. Just think of the Caracal case and how badly that was handled. The Behavioural Analysis Unit never even showed up. I don't know if they were even involved. But there was quite a media storm, which is understandable, since the kidnapped girl managed to call 112 and they couldn't save her. For two days the newspapers kept speculating that she was kept hidden somewhere, but she was already dead, as we now know.'

'So in fact you are trying to reform the police?'

'You're being sarcastic and there's no need for that. I really think we need experts. These cases might be few and far between, but we can't just rely on that. We can't just accept failure because it only happens every few years. I believe we shouldn't fail any victim.'

'I hear what you're saying and I agree somewhat. I know you contributed quite a bit to the case with the crazy psychiatrist, but I want to take this institution in another direction. Maybe make it a real institute.'

'OK. But I will require your support in what I do next, both for my collaboration with the police and for my doctorate. I will continue to be involved in all the serious cases, rare though they might be. And I will head off to Groningen to discuss my thesis with my supervisor every now and then. I don't know how long that will take – maybe just three years, maybe more, but I really want to do this.'

'Fine, do as you wish. What I need from you right now is to attend this conference today. And, since it looks like you won't leave my office until I do so, I can promise you that you have my support.'

**

'Good morning, Aphrodite.'

'Good morning, Matei – although morning was a few hours ago. Did you miss me that much that you had to call me on my first day back at work?' Gigi laughed.

'Welcome back, get out of bed, we've got work to do!'

'I'm not in bed, I'm at work. I got here at seven because I missed it so much. What happened?'

'You have to come and see. The car is on its way.'

'Give me ten minutes to let my director know. Besides, I need to go to a conference this afternoon.'

'Ten minutes tops. We'll bring you back, but I want you to see things before we move the body.'

'I'll be ready, but what are we talking about?'

'Less talk, more action. We can discuss it here.'

She went to the lockers to get changed and then went back to Lemnaru's office.

'I'm sorry, it's an urgent matter, I need to go out for an hour or two.'

'What for?'

'The police called me, they're sending a car, they didn't

want to discuss it over the phone. It was Chief Inspector Matei Vălean, I need to go.'

'Gigi, don't let me down with that conference or I will be really furious!'

'I'll be back in time, sir, I promise!'

**

She didn't know the driver.

'Good morning, I am Gigi Alexa, please call me Gigi.'

'Yes, Dr Alexa, I will try. I am PC Nicu Mocanu.'

'What's happening? Can you tell me anything?'

'No, I'm sorry. The Chief Inspector warned me you'd ask but told me to keep my mouth shut no matter how hard you try.'

'No chance of persuading you, then?...'

'Not a chance, Dr Alexa. But we'll get there soon enough, it's still quiet at this time of day, still holiday season.'

On the street all you could see were the police cars. Matei threw away his cigarette when he saw Gigi and opened the car door for her.

'Morning.'

'It's certainly not a good one,' Gigi said, hugging him.

'You ain't seen nothing yet. I'd like to warn you, the victim looks a bit like you, that's why I called you and wanted to be here with you.'

'What do you mean?'

'She was the actress Andrada Vasiliu, you might know her.'

'I've heard of her. I've never seen her.'

'Not even the poster? The first time I saw it in town, I thought it was you '

'Ah, yes, Radu showed me. She doesn't look at all like me.'

'It's the hair, Gigi. The facial traits might be different, but when you see that big mop of curly blonde hair... you have to admit it's not that common.'

'That's like saying that two people who wear the same hat resemble each other. Or two brunettes, or two redheads. Why blondes?'

'It's not just the colour, Gigi, but also the shape of it. You know what I mean.'

'Fine. Let's go in.'

She spotted the body from the gate. Four members of the forensic team were standing between the gate and the front door. They stepped aside and she saw the body, lying down on one side, her blonde hair covering her face. She was completely naked, the hands bent with the palms facing downwards in front of her. The knees were flexed and she seemed to be slightly stretched. Her skin was lightly tanned.

'Is this how you found her?'

'Yes, I had a shock. Although I know your address, at first sight I thought it might have been you.'

'You exaggerate, no need to worry so much.'

'It's a strange business. The man who found the body was walking his dog. He said the gate was half-open and he went in after his dog. I haven't moved anything.'

'Time of death?'

'Around one in the morning. I think the dog caused her to fall.'

'What do you mean?'

'I think she was posed as if crouching, on her knees, with her arms stretched out and her head on the arms. You know that expression...'

'Like a dog brought to heel?'

'Yes, it sounds crazy, but...'

'Her clothes?'

'We're looking for them.'

'Is the house open?'

'No. And her keys are in the handbag. She either managed to enter the garden and the killer followed her, or else he attacked her at the gate, just as she was unlocking it.'

'Neighbours?'

'Nothing yet. My colleagues are knocking on doors, but no one heard anything.'

Gigi took a pair of gloves from Matei and bent over the body. The curly hair was almost the exact same colour as hers. The roots were slightly darker and there were a few white hairs too. She sensed a sickly-sweet smell.

'Chloroform.'

'Yes,' Matei confirmed it.

The body wasn't fully rigid yet. She gently brushed the hair aside and saw a pair of blue eyes looking straight at her. There were a few big bruises on her neck.

'Any chance of fingerprints? Have you tried?'

'No.'

'She doesn't seem to have been sexually assaulted. The strangling must have been very rapid, and then he posed her. I don't think it took more than 15 minutes in all. Did you see this?' Gigi pointed at the index finger of the right hand.

'What?'

'Her nail is missing.'

'Torn off.'

'Yes, I don't think she was alive when the killer did that. Which means that the killer must have stayed beside her at least for half an hour until there was no more bleeding, bearing in mind that it was about 20 degrees last night. There aren't any CCTV cameras around, are there?'

'No,' sighed Matei.

'We need to check the side streets.'

'There are too many of them. He could have taken any route. Even headed off towards the forest and then back to the centre of town. But yes, we'll check everything we can.'

'What do you know about her?'

'I like your relentless interrogation. No need to frown, I'll reply even if you get annoying. I want you in on this case. She lived alone. This is her parents' house, but they've moved to the countryside.'

'Have you spoken to them?'

'No, I'm waiting for Paul to unlock her phone.'

'Have you got approval?'

'Don't need to wait for it. That's the beauty of Paul, he has already been sentenced and is serving his sentence by helping us out. I think in about half an hour we should have access to all the numbers.'

'Oh, because everyone saves their Mum's number under 'Mum' on their phone?'

'We'll see.'

'Anything else?'

'Not much. She seems to have been single for some time. I checked out her Facebook, nothing interesting. We might have to hack into her profile there.'

'Can't you just ask for permission to access it?'

'Not even her mother would be given access, except if she told Facebook that her daughter had died. Even so, she might not see all her messages and posts except if they were friends. You're not on FB, are you?'

'No intention of doing that, don't need it.'

'I can't say I blame you.'

'Do you have a FB profile?'

'Yes, I set one up last year.'

'Your real name? With picture and everything?'

'Yes.'

'Why on earth? What made you do that?'

'No need to go into details...'

'Ah yes, you had a Tinder profile too, I seem to remember. But I thought that now you've been made a Chief Inspector, you might have become more cautious. Besides, you have a girlfriend, are you still with her?'

'We met two months ago and I told you then that we were still together, don't pretend you've forgotten. Yes, we're together and things are going well. And you know full well her name is Alina. Stop the chit-chat and see if there's anything else you need here. If not, then we should take her body to the Institute.'

Gigi took him aside and whispered in his ear: 'Please tell them to leave.'

'Why?'

'I want to check if she was indeed initially in the position that you said.'

'You have to suit up, then.'

Matei had been right. They straightened her up and she seemed stable. The body was still not entirely cold and felt strange to touch. Gigi was used to the ice-cold corpses at the morgue, and this was an entirely different sensation. Aside from the smell of chloroform, a heavy and sweet perfume emanated from the young woman.

'Are you OK?'

Gigi's eyes were swimming, and she had a knot in her throat.

The residual warmth of the corpse had brought it all so much closer, like a whisper growing ever fainter, ever harder to perceive. The dead cannot talk, yet they always tell us the truth.

'I told you it was different at the crime scene,' Matei put a hand on her arm.

'Yes, by the time they reach me, it's obvious that nothing more can be done for them. But here it feels too close. She was just outside her house. A little further and she might have escaped. Who do you think might be the killer?'

'I really haven't a clue. It feels personal.'

'You don't think she was picked at random?'

'They didn't even bother to make it look like a robbery.'

'They certainly spent some time staging it, but I'm not sure what message the perpetrator meant to convey. I will have a report for you after the autopsy.'

'Since you're part of the Behavioural Analysis Unit.' Matei bowed ironically.

'The first case since it was founded. Thanks for calling me here.' Gigi bowed too.

'I think we can safely say that it is a strange case, that's why I got you involved. Can you handle it on your own, or do you need to get help from Bucharest?'

'I need to inform them, obviously.'

'Believe me, I envy you.'

'What for?'

'For the special unit, for being able to intervene in our cases as you please. If Tomescu hadn't been there, none of this would have happened.'

Gigi's temper flared up. 'We solved the Fora case together, Matei – don't forget that!'

'Just saying, not trying to annoy anyone. And I do want us to work together.'

'I'll deal with this tomorrow. I told you I have to go to a conference this afternoon. It's complicated. Lemnaru wants me to go, I can't refuse. I'll go to the office and pick up my presentation on the memory stick, then go home and change. It's a urology conference, don't act so surprised.'

'What have you got to do with that?'

'Emil was supposed to go, but he is on annual leave. Come on, I don't have time for all this. It's all ego and nonsense. The director wants us to promote the institute and our expertise.'

She left Matei chuckling, then turned back to say: 'By the way, I'll take Nicu to drive me back.'

**

It was only four in the afternoon of her first day back at work, but the holiday already felt like a distant memory. Gigi got out of the taxi and headed into the hotel. Aro Palace had been opened in the late 1930s, with some pomp and circumstance. The new wing, which resembled a block of flats, had been tagged on some twenty years ago, and the whole building was currently the only five-star hotel in Braşov. In the past, there had been a fountain right in front of the hotel where now there was a kind of glass pyramid providing a glimpse of the swimming pool in the basement. Gigi had always wondered what it would be like to dip her feet in the water. Except that, even back in those days, before the fountain had been replaced by the pyramid, she wouldn't have been able to get to it without walking on the grass, and there were at least two big signs saying 'Forbidden to step on the grass'. That Romanian obsession with keeping any green spaces pristine.

The décor inside was a muddle of too many styles, with no clear intent to unify the marble floors, the polished wood and brass bars on the stairs. The two ladies at reception completely ignored Gigi. She looked around and decided the conference rooms must be on the first floor. A poster at the foot of the stairs confirmed that, so she went up. The conference had started. She was stopped at the door by a young woman with long black hair, which she kept fluffing up every minute or so, then pulling a strand towards her chest to straighten it. Gigi looked her in the eyes:

'I need to get in, I'm one of the speakers.'

'If you're not on the list, I can't do anything about it.'

'As I just told you, my colleague Dr Emil Sandu is on the list, from the County Service for Forensic Medicine. I'm replacing him.'

'We were not informed of that.'

'Who's we?'

'The organisers.'

'Are you a student, young lady?'

'Yes, second year.'

'So you've only just finished the first year, right?'

'Yes.'

'OK, so you still have five years to go. Please try and understand me. I've just got back from holiday, it's my first day at work and my boss sent me here. My boss thinks it's important for us to take part. I don't agree, but I don't have any say in it. I could leave right now, but it would create a huge scandal. If I tell him that I was prevented from going inside by you, I don't know what he would do. Given that he's a lecturer at your university, I'd say it's not worth the risk.'

Gigi was usually courteous with people she didn't know, using the polite form for verbs and pronouns, but she knew that some people reacted better to the blunt approach. Yes, she was intimidating this girl, but she'd get over it. The student stopped playing with her hair for a moment, then gestured to Gigi that she should go in.

The meeting room was darkened, all Gigi could see was the cross-section of kidneys projected onto the screen. A buxom woman was speaking in a monotone at the front of the room. Gigi tiptoed across, so as not to wake anybody up. Most of the audience members were looking at their phones and ignoring the presentation. Anyone who bores an audience that much deserves every punishment. They should never get up on stage again if they have nothing to say and aren't capable of sparking the interest of the audience. Gigi managed to find a free seat, in the middle of the front row. The speaker frowned at her, perhaps that was her seat. Never mind. The man sitting to her left smiled at her. Gigi was sure she didn't know him. Around forty, dark, with a side parting, and the face of a movie star.

'Hello, I am Lucian Conrad, urologist.'

'Hello, Gigi Alexa, pathologist,' she said, shaking his hand and seeing the look of surprise in his eyes.

'You're one of the speakers, right?'

'Yes, I might be next, actually. I came here instead of Dr Emil Sandu.'

'Good luck.'

The speaker finally finished and the audience realised they were supposed to clap when they saw the final slide with two hands and a neon 'Thank You'. The lights went on and the man next to her jumped up as if he were on springs.

'Thank you, Dr Amalia Baiulescu, that was very interesting. Any questions?'

The audience fidgeted in their seats, but no one commented at all.

'In that case, allow me to invite Dr Regina Alexa from the County Service for Forensic Medicine to the stage. I am delighted that we are starting a collaboration. I am sure you will bring much new and relevant information.'

Gigi smiled and nodded. There was no applause.

'Good afternoon. Please believe me that this change of programme was as much of a surprise for me as it was for you. I was only told about this conference this morning. The presentation has been put together by my colleague Emil Sandu. So, if you find the information interesting, I'll take the credit, and if you get bored, I'll blame my colleague.'

She was expecting to get at least a couple of smiles, maybe even a chuckle or two, but the audience remained impassive, most likely asleep. Of course, women who make such jokes when presenting are not considered as amusing as the men who do so; women appear weak, while men appear brilliantly humble. Nevertheless, she ploughed on.

'Before I start telling you about this fascinating case of a person whose single kidney was only discovered during an autopsy, I'd like to add something to what Dr Baiulescu just said. Those patients who've been diagnosed with Fabry disease should have as much information as possible about their condition in case they decide to have children. It is a painful disease and you might want to think twice before passing it on. A father can only pass the disease on to his daughters, but it gets more complicated when we're dealing with the mother, who can pass it on to either sex. Chorionic villus sampling can be performed early in the pregnancy, at 10-12 weeks, so before amniocentesis, but it can double the risk of miscarriage. Current legislation allows women to decide to keep or discard their embryo up to the twelfth week, but we know that in practice abortions can take place later. For example, amniocentesis is regularly performed between weeks 15-20. I think it would be ethical to prioritise the mother's needs over that of the unborn infant, and that we should be more honest about this type of information. I have no doubt that in the future more genetic testing will become available. And since couples are having problems conceiving naturally, many of those tests will be performed directly during IVF, checking embryo viability but also leading possibly to embryo modification. These procedures will be extremely expensive, of course, which will exacerbate the gap between the wealthy and the poor. Rich people will be increasingly healthy and up-to-date, while the poor will be less and less healthy.'

Everybody stopped to stare at her, she could feel it. They all seemed to be holding their collective breath. Why did she have to open her mouth? She turned back towards the screen and started her presentation without any further personal comments. There were no questions at the end. She was the final speaker and everyone was impatient for the session to finish so that they could go for dinner.

**

'I thought that was remarkably brave of you.'

Lucian Conrad came up to her while she was tidying up her notes. 'Will you join us for dinner?'

'I'm sorry, I have to rush home, but thank you for the invitation.'

'I'm pretty sure the participants would have asked some questions if they hadn't been so concerned about their dinner.'

'You think so? What about?'

'About your opinions. For example, what you might have

to say about transplants.'

'Why, do you think that my opinions might be different from theirs?'

'I might be jumping to conclusions. But, for example, I don't think transplants should be given automatically to just anybody.'

'You mean there should be some selection criteria? If I'm not mistaken, there are such criteria and they are applied, are they not?'

'Yes, but they don't take into account all the factors.'

'I'm sorry, I don't understand...'

'I meant that we need to do more extensive testing to make sure that our waiting lists are responsibly compiled.'

'Possibly. I tend to spend my time with those who were not on the waiting lists or did not receive help in time.'

'Are you always this cynical?'

'I believe so. Professional hazard, got to have a black sense of humour.'

They both laughed and Dr Conrad accompanied her to the door.

'Well, I hope we'll meet again. I've recently moved to Braşov and am delighted to meet interesting people here.'

'Thank you. We might meet at the next conference. But only if my colleague tricks me again.'

She texted Radu as soon as she got in the cab.

What a day I've had! They sent me to present at a conference. I feel like the solitary kidney I had to talk about... I did my best. I wasn't expecting to miss you so much. No matter how well I cope on my own, sometimes it's simply better with the two of us.

He replied:

Raul gave your haircut to one of his clients, my dear lioness. He did his best, but you are of course unique, my sweet. Although it's lions who have the mane, not lionesses, of course.

My hair colour is lighter, Nea Pavel told me this morning, I hadn't even noticed. I miss you so much!

Three more days. I've been searching for you all my life, I think I can last that long.
Stop being so sickly sweet...

3

Gigi slept badly. She woke up before the cat. Unheard of. She dragged herself to the kitchen and started the coffee machine. Of course, she had to throw out the dregs, then she had to refill the water, two extra trips, but what could she do. Ten seconds delay until she could get her fix. She only went to the toilet after she had started the machine. On the way there, she nearly fell over Morty, who was stretched across the full width of the corridor.

'Idiot, get out of the way!'

She spoke to him all the time. Sometimes even when Radu was around, who said it was a bad habit to mutter to yourself. She said she wasn't talking to herself but to her cat. Besides, there were studies proving that geniuses often talked to themselves. The problem wasn't talking aloud, but starting to hear voices answering back.

Matei had worried that the physical resemblance might shock her, but that hadn't been the case. What had upset her – and she realised it only when she left the place yesterday – was the sense of emptiness, of waste, endless pity and an undefined sense of fear. The fear was because she had no idea what had happened there and the pity was because she hoped that the woman hadn't suffered too much. Sometimes Gigi wondered if she was a psychopath – she seemed to miss some basic human feelings. Or perhaps they weren't missing, they were simply very much delayed. She had this capacity for numbing her emotions for a while.

**

The young woman had completely lost her golden shine once she was on the examination table. Gigi tied up her hair so she could examine the neck injuries, which were the likely cause of death. The attacker had surprised her with the chloroform, so she might not have felt a thing. There were no other signs of violence. Gigi took off her gloves to answer the phone.

'What's up. Matei?'

'We found her clothes.'

'Where?'

'Further up on the street. Dress, underwear, sandals. About ten metres from the house, covered by grass.'

'Any traces?'

'Nothing significant, the ground was completely dry. When is your report ready?'

'In two-three hours. I'll send it. I don't know how they pulled off the fingernail.'

'What is so special about that?'

'It was done very cleanly. The perpetrator was strong and had the right tool for the job.'

'Like a pair of pliers?'

'Something better than that. She had false nails, and the perpetrator was careful to grip both the false and the real nail and pull them off.'

'See you at the station later?'

'I'll be there with the report and I'll bring some photos too.'

The door opened slowly and the technician stuck her head in.

'Dr Alexa, there is someone for you at the entrance.'

'For me?'

'Yes, a courier. He says you have to sign for it.'

A young man stood in the entrance hall holding a giant bouquet of tulips.

'Ms Regina Alexa?'

'That's me?'

She was so surprised that her answer sounded like a question.

'You know best. This bouquet is for you.'

'Thank you. Where are they from?'

'From Luxury Flowers.'

'I mean, who are they from?'

'I don't know, ma'am, there's no note. Which means I have no information about who ordered them.'

'Fine, thanks.'

The red tulips were tied with a white ribbon. The card attached was simply the card from the flower shop. The technician came up to her.

'They're so beautiful, Dr Alexa. Do you want me to put them in your office?'

'Laura, I've asked you so many times to call me by my first name.'

'I know, Dr Alexa, maybe someday I'll be able to, but I've only been here for a month.'

'How come you decided to join us, by the way?'

'They pay well and it's regular office hours. I live in Moeciu and commute, so I can help my family. I like it here.'

'I see. Well, take the flowers and put them in water, thank you.'

She took out her phone and texted.

Hi. Horror. Remember the theatre poster you kept showing me all over town? With the actress you said resembled me? Her name is Andrada Vasiliu and she was on my dissection table just now. She was found yesterday. I'm so upset that I nearly forgot to tell you, but no doubt the press will be all over it. Thanks for the flowers, they cheered me up. Miss you, come home soon.

What flowers?

A bouquet of tulips. Aren't they from you? Luxury Flowers.

My love, please take care. I didn't send anything. I'll be home in two days.

**

Did you send me flowers?
She could see Matei typing, deleting, typing again.
U crazy? No. What flowers?
Tulips.
WTF?
Talk later.

**

She hadn't texted him in ages. He was the one who would send the occasional standard message: 'Have a good week' or 'Wishing you a nice weekend.' She only ever replied 'Thanks'. She never even opened them up fully or asked him how he was doing in Bucharest.

Morning. Thank you for the flowers, in case you sent them.
This time it's someone else. But thanks for thinking of me.
If it wasn't Vlad either, then who on earth could it be?

**

Gigi had an access card now and no longer needed to sign in at the gate at the police station. She went up to the large meeting room on the first floor, where Matei was summarising the case thus far. The photos of the crime scene were prominently displayed on a board, with question marks around them.

'Andrada Vasiliu's parents have just got here. I went to speak with them myself. They will identify the body tomorrow. Gigi, I hope it will be ready by then?'

'Yes, no problem, I'll be there too.'

Matei looked at her and said, 'Please tie up your hair or something, if you meet with them.'

'Ah, yes, I see. I've actually let Radu know for the same reason. Thought he might stumble on her picture somewhere in the news and, since you keep insisting how much she looks like me... What did her parents say?'

'Nothing much. They moved to the countryside a few years ago, and Andrada was living alone, had no significant other in her life. It's fairly clear how the murder was done: sedation and then strangulation. But we have no motive. As for opportunity, obviously: late at night, quiet residential neighbourhood. We haven't been able to find out anything from the neighbours, no CCTV in the area, although some of the houses had home security cameras installed. On one of them, a few houses further down, we see Andrada Vasiliu passing at quarter to one. The attacker seems to have avoided it, the camera only points towards the gate. Either he was aware of it, or he got lucky, but he never appears on it. And the images are pretty unclear anyway. Have you got anything to add, Gigi?'

'Very little. The attacker must have been quite strong, at least 180 cm tall. I assume he covered her face with chloroform at the gate, then carried her through into the garden, where he turned her to face him and strangled her. There are fibres in her oral cavity, probably some kind of gauze or bandage. 100% cotton. Nothing special. You should check to see if there are traces on the wall, where he propped her up as he strangled her. If so, there might be some fibres from his clothing on the walls of the house.'

'Any profiling possible?'

'Too little data, but I would say an adult man in his prime, well-built. That's all as far as physical description goes. It was almost certainly premeditated. He must have followed her several nights in a row, knew her habits, knew the area. You should check any previous recordings on the private security cameras, day-time ones as well. Or ask the neighbours if they saw anyone hanging around. What did Andrada do that evening?'

'She was in a show at the Reduta Theatre. Her own adaptation of Medea by Euripides, transformed into a one-woman show,' said Marcel Aurescu, standing up. 'I spoke to the theatre director, it was an independent production organised by her. All alone on stage, with a few projections. That evening, after the show, they all went to have a drink at the restaurant opposite. They left at around midnight. Nothing out of the common. Andrada Vasiliu walked home by herself. She hadn't drunk much.'

'Confirmed. Her blood alcohol levels were 0.037%, so she had had at most two glasses of wine,' said Gigi.

'Regarding the play, any rivalries, or anything?' asked Matei.

'The director said no. She had no enemies, no furious exes that they knew of. Her last relationship had been with an actor from Bucharest, but that was at least two years ago. Since then, nothing.'

'So no clear leads. I'll try the parents again tomorrow, when they come to the morgue,' said Matei, looking down.

'All we can do is search the area again and see if there are any other images. Were there any footprints on the terrace?'

'Not even partials. The terrace was sparkling clean, probably had been washed recently. Nothing helpful there.'

'We have to find a motive.'

'I know,' said Matei, his head still hanging.

'Are you thinking what I'm thinking?'

'If you're thinking that we're in a great big hole, then yes. I'll get a statement from her former lover, we can talk to colleagues in Bucharest, but I don't think we'll get any new leads.'

'Didn't she have any friends?'

'We'll talk to all of them. Let's go home now.'

'Do you want to have a drink with us?' Alina Moise, the police spokesperson and Matei's girlfriend, was waiting in front of the office.

'No thanks, I'm too tired. I'd like the script of the play if possible.'

'To do what, Gigi?'

'Read it. Maybe I'll find something there.'

'OK, I'll ask Marcel to find it and send it to you. Take care of yourself.'

'Thanks, have a nice evening.'

Alina waved and smiled at her. These relationships at work should be forbidden. There would be such a scandal when Matei got tired of her. But that was none of her business, Gigi decided. Matei could do exactly as he pleased.

4

The Second

The computer switched off abruptly. She had forgotten to switch the light on, the glow from the screen had been enough. She was wasting her time, she was unable to do any serious work, but she had simply lost track of time. She had been filling in an order form and now would have to start all over again, unless something had been saved automatically.

She looked up and noticed that night had fallen outside. This was the third power cut in a single evening. She had spent the whole week trying to identify where the problem was but was unable to find it. As if a child was playing with the switch. She was tired and wanted to go to bed. She had been on her feet all day long.

He was watching her from the other side of the street, waiting for her to finish. There were people waiting at the bus stop, but he didn't sit down next to them. He was sitting a little further on and could see the dimly-lit hairdressing salon. When the lights went out, he crossed the street quickly and waited outside the door.

She jumped when she heard the thudding knock. She stood up and saw that there was a man standing in front of the door to the shop, his face slightly hidden. She opened the door and poked out her head only.

'Can I help you?'

'I know it's late but I wanted to make an appointment for tomorrow.'

'Best to call tomorrow morning. I can't help you now, there's been a power cut.'

'Please, madam a friend recommended you.'

'Come by tomorrow.'

'OK, I understand. Can you at least give me a phone number, if you don't mind?'

'I'll give you a card.'

She stepped back in and stumbled, trying to feel her way to the display on the reception desk where she kept her business cards. She didn't hear him behind her. When she turned, she saw that he had already stepped inside.

'Apologies, I don't want to scare you, but I couldn't see you, so I came in.'

The man started walking up and down the shop.

'It's very nice here.'

'Thank you. I can't find the cards, maybe my colleagues have moved them. I'll give you my number.'

She went to get her bag from the room in the back, and returned holding it, searching for her mobile phone.

'I was planning to go home about an hour ago, but then I started doing some online orders. I can't find my phone. I thought it was here.'

'Why do you need it?'

'I wanted to use the torch, it's too dark in here.'

'I've got one,' he said, moving closer.

Something about his movements put her on the alert. She sat down and opened the drawer, trying to get something from inside. He moved in and, with a sudden gesture, he wrapped something around her neck. The scream died in her throat. She should never have opened that door.

5

Gigi reached out her hand to stop her phone ringing. She was doing the afternoon shift, so she had switched her alarm off. Which meant it was urgent.

'Matei, what on earth couldn't wait until the afternoon?'

'We've got another body. I want you there.'

'What?'

'A robbery at a hairdresser's. Maybe I'm being paranoid. Anyway, best get over here and give me your opinion. We're on high alert at the moment, so I'm going to be calling you out on any homicide, whether related or not to the actress.'

'Are you sending a car?'

'It's on its way.'

**

Nicu handed her a cup of coffee as soon she got into the passenger seat.

'The Chief Inspector told me things would be easier if I gave you some coffee.'

'Thanks. I know you're not to blame. Where are we headed?'

'Calea Bucureşti.'

'What's there?'

'A hairdresser.'

'Can you give me any further details?'

'Sorry, I haven't been there yet myself. All I know is that the owner was found by the cleaner this morning, about half an hour ago.'

There was only one police car parked outside, plus the forensic team's van. Gigi reached the doorway and Matei gesticulated that she should get kitted out first. The photographer was still taking pictures. She quickly donned her coveralls and hood.

'You look like a ghost,' said Matei.

'Good morning to you too. What's the issue, why did you call me?'

'Irina Oprea. Hairdresser and owner. The cleaning lady dialled 112. She came in and found Irina sleeping with her head on the desk, or so she thought. When she touched her, she was cold and the cleaner got a fright.'

'Where is the cleaning lady?'

'At the back, Marcel is taking her statement.'

'When did you get here?'

'Twenty minutes ago, we moved fast.'

'Estimated time of death?'

'Last night, maybe ten.'

'Witnesses?'

'Are you interrogating me again?'

'Well, if you don't tell me things...'

'Fine then. The woman was living alone. 52 years old, her son is nearly 30 and lives in Italy. That's what I learned from the cleaner. She had a few friends, all seemed to be going well. She would often stay late at the shop. She has two employees, one for each shift.'

'At least here we have CCTV cameras.'

'Yes, except there was a power cut. The attacker must have taken advantage of that. And there was no back-up power option. I don't know why people only do things half-heartedly.'

'Because she was probably using the CCTV to check on her employees, not for protection. We are a very suspicious nation. Do you think she was being stalked?'

'Couldn't tell you.'

'How was she killed?'

'Strangled with a belt from here.'

'Is there anything missing?'

'The metal box with the day's earnings. It was in the top drawer.'

'Anything else?'

'No.'

'Any fingerprints?'

'None. I think it was only made to look like a robbery.'

'Don't you think you might be exaggerating?'

'I can't help it.'

'Why are you grinning like a fool?'

'I can tell you, because you're as crazy as me. I just find it all quite exciting.'

'Don't you think that is somewhat inhumane?'

'Look who's talking, Deathwitch!'

'You're so fucked up.'

'That's why we get on. It's a real challenge, a case like this. Or the two cases. The previous one is equally exciting.'

'Have you found out anything more about that one?'

'No. I spoke to my colleagues in Bucharest, those who interrogated the ex-boyfriend. He was returning from Greece that very day and stayed over at his new girlfriend's house. He hadn't been in touch with Andrada since they broke up.'

'OK, coming back to this case. Why do you think they might be related?'

'It's just a gut feeling.'

'Or your desire to have a sensational case. You said they took nothing else. Did they search the place at least?'

'They did. All the drawers were open, here and in the back room. They even went into the bathroom. So we have a footprint this time.'

'Anything special about the footprint?'

'No, a trainer, seems fairly common. Roughly size 44. Since this is a ladies' hairdresser... I suppose they washed the floor before closing and there are no other prints. But that's not necessarily proof of anything.'

'So why did you call me?'

'I want you to take a closer look. Come here, the boys have finished now.'

What had looked like a bun was in fact a short ponytail, hacked off around the elastic that was holding it in place. The rest of the woman's head was covered in cornrow braids. Gigi looked up at Matei.

'Where's the rest of the hair?'

'In the bin. Look.' Matei showed her the rubbish bin under the desk, which was filled to the brim with cut-off cornrows.

'I see. This is really strange. All the more since it appears to be an opportunistic attack, unless you think he was the one cutting off the electricity.'

'Doubt it. They've got building works in the area and have had frequent power cuts. The longest one was at ten yesterday evening.'

'Matei, I have to let Bucharest know. Even if we aren't sure the cases are linked.'

'Two crimes in three days. It is exciting, isn't it? Tomescu will come. I think he would have anyway.'

'How do you know?'

'I spoke to him last night. I think he trod on some sensitive toes over there and may be contemplating a return to Braşov.'

'Great,' Gigi scowled.

'Have you talked to him?'

'No. He sends me a message now and then, but we've never really spoken.'

'He was always on your side.'

'Are you being jealous or ironic?'

'Just saying: if it weren't for him, you wouldn't be here.'

'You know that I'm good at my job. No need to go over this again. You said something like this yesterday too. I thought we were good mates.'

'I'm a country lad who had to work very hard for everything, never got anything handed to me on a plate. So yes, I was a little envious, I don't mind admitting that.'

He looked down, as if checking to see if his shoelaces were tied properly. He was right, it hadn't been easy for him as a boy born in one of the poorest houses in his village of Brad in Bacău county. He could be proud of what he'd accomplished. She smiled at him, took a hand out of the pocket of her yellow skirt with big red flowers and tapped him gently on the shoulder.

'Matei, I hope we can be friends. All going well with Alina?'

'Yes, why do you keep asking? She's very committed. We are discussing moving in together. It will probably be fine. She knows what this job is like. And you?'

'We're fine.'

'Maybe we can all go out together at some point.'

'I'm asocial. I simply don't like having people around me.'

'I'm the same. Never mind. Do you think you can do the autopsy today? Shall we have a case update in the afternoon at around four?'

'Yes, I'll send you the report asap and see if I can find out anything more by then.'

**

The first time she'd seen her, the similarity did not seem that obvious. But now, when Gigi pulled aside the white cloth and saw Andrada's peaceful face, she felt a wave of nausea. She grabbed the metal edge of the table and held on tight. She had combed the hair, disguised the bruises around the neck a little for the sake of the parents. The identification was the toughest part of the job. She was quite resilient usually, but when faced with those waves of grief, they seemed to wash right over her. She could control her own emotions, even ignore them, but when she came face to face with other people's emotions, she couldn't help being infected. She usually tried to hide it by wearing more make-up and blusher than usual, to mask a deathly pallor matching the corpse's.

She had the brainwave to fasten her hair back in a pony-tail and hide her fringe with a wide hairband, pulled over her forehead. That way, the resemblance was less striking.

She went out into the hallway and saw the mother walking towards her, bent over, holding tight onto the elbow of the father, who was walking slightly more upright. He was dragging his leg, and Gigi couldn't help wondering if it was an old problem or if he had suffered a minor stroke upon hearing the bad news. She furtively examined his arm movements and decided not to ask.

'Good afternoon. I am Dr Regina Alexa. This way, please. I am so sorry for your loss.'

They went to her office first. They were unable to say anything. They couldn't even look her in the face. She sat down.

'We'll go to the autopsy room and I'll pull back the sheet slowly.'

'But why, why?'

'I am so sorry, Mrs Vasiliu. We don't have an answer yet.'

'Are you trying to catch him too?'

'Yes, I promise.'

'Elena, let's get it over with. No point in prolonging the pain. We have so much to do now.'

She made sure to enter the room first. She went up to the autopsy table and signalled that they should draw near. She gently opened the zipper, and Elena Vasiliu's breath could no longer be heard. Gigi felt her feet turn icy cold, but she gripped the protective cloth with one hand and lifted it to show the face. Elena stepped forward and asked with her eyes if she could touch the body. Gigi nodded, and stepped back. Elena whimpered, barely audible, then she clutched the table and said: 'Yes, that's our girl.'

'I am so sorry, Mrs Vasiliu, what happened is so terrible.'

The father had remained near the doorway throughout. He was leaning against the back of a chair and waiting for his wife to rejoin him, then they left the lab together. Gigi did up the zipper and followed them.

'When can we pick her up?'

'Soon, I hope.' Gigi resisted the impulse to give the mother a hug. 'If there is anything else I can do to help, let me know.'

'Dr Alexa, there's nothing more you can do. Neither can we. Such grief won't go away soon. I don't even know if I want to carry on. My life has ended.'

'Mr Vasiliu, I know this is horrible. I just wanted to say that I am here if you need to talk about it with anyone.'

'I just want to find out who did this.'

'I promise you that there are many of us working on this case and we won't rest until we find the perpetrator.'

The elderly couple left, their feet shuffling against the tiles. Gigi went back to her office, her teeth and fists clenched tight. She poured herself a glass of water, but it tasted bitter.

6

The Third

He should have taken his car – the other passengers on the near-empty bus were staring at his runner's get-up. He decided to ignore them and wondered instead which of the two cable cars might be working. Out of season, only one of them was functional, either the one near Capra Neagrǎ restaurant or the one next to the gondola lift. The day had started well, bright, with very clear skies.

A motley crowd was going up to the Poiana Braşov resort: some heading for work in the few open and practically empty hotels, three or four hikers, two families with kids. He had plenty of time to check them out in the 30 minutes or so that it took to get there from Braşov. He wondered if he should head back down on foot in the afternoon, instead of taking the bus. He'd think about it. Maybe he'd sit a while sunning himself at the Postǎvaru Chalet. But first he would climb up to the peak.

He was proud of his physical fitness. Although he was over fifty years old, he was still very active. He ran three times a week around the track at the PE college, and climbed up and down Postǎvaru Mountain at least once a week.

He felt a small moment of personal triumph when he guessed correctly which cable car would be working. He bought a one-way ticket. The cold draught on the stairs left a metallic taste in his mouth. On the platform there was a group of weekend tourists, probably from Bucharest or somewhere down south, wearing city clothes, jeans, shirts, dresses. Three couples. They were bound to strut about at the summit, exclaiming loudly over the mountains they could neither identify nor name, taking lots of selfies. He tried to hide his disdain by putting on his sunglasses. He had been born in this town and had nothing but contempt for people who did not respect the mountains. As soon as it got warm, the trails were overrun with them.

When the cable car arrived, he greeted the boy operating the controls without waiting for a reply and headed into the far corner. He could admire the beautiful landscape even through the scratched window. He saw a fox to the right of the shed housing the snow cannons, and hoped he would meet it when coming down. It would be better to take this route instead of Lupului − the Wolf Piste. In winter he preferred skiing down that one. He liked to take a day off, usually Mondays, but even better on a Wednesday. The slopes were empty outside the school holidays. Poiana had too few ski slopes to be a desirable resort throughout the winter.

He quickly left the other tourists behind and headed for his preferred spot, which offered a panoramic view of Predeal. He could see the Bucegi mountains in the distance and sat down to admire the landscape. It was a little routine he had every time he got up here, and he was happy to be alone.

He heard some voices behind him and he turned around angrily, thinking those vulgar tourists had followed him, but they were heading in a different direction. He breathed a sigh of relief, stood up and searched for his water bottle in the backpack. He lifted it up to drink, but a strange sound made him jump, spilling some water onto himself. Someone was breathing heavily behind him, but he had no time to see anything more.

The man – it must have been a man to push him with such force – had gathered all his strength to give him a shove. The pain he felt in his back and the sensation of floating above the valley were almost instantaneous. As he fell, he tried to grasp at the branches of the pine trees, but he failed. He had often watched crows executing their aerial manoeuvres with breathless admiration. Now he thought he would like to be reincarnated as a crow, if he didn't survive this fall.

7

The room was in darkness. Gigi picked up her phone and saw it was seven in the morning. The alarm hadn't gone off because she had switched it off. She stretched her body out again. The new bedroom curtains blocked the light well, and she had also closed the shutters throughout the house. That's why she thought it was earlier than it was.

Last night, on her way home, she had looked over her shoulder constantly. She couldn't shake off the feeling that someone was behind her.

Although the streets were lit, there were places drowned in shadows from the still leafy trees. She thought she heard footsteps behind her, but when she turned around, she couldn't see anybody. She crossed the road, since the pavement was wider on the other side. As she passed by the military barracks at the end of the street she stopped and bent over to tie her shoelaces. That's when she caught a glimpse of something, a distant shadow hovering just in the corner of her eye. Her heartbeat quickened and she started searching desperately in her handbag for her phone. The shadow turned into a side street and she could breathe easily once more.

Maybe the mention of Vlad Tomescu had been enough to put her on her guard. She didn't want him around.

Back home, she had sat up late to read the play. Matei had given her the script he had acquired from the play's director. Andrada Vasiliu had come with the text of the play, he had simply helped her to stage it. He had told Matei that it was a manifesto against domestic violence.

Gigi thought she might know something about that.

Her mother was an alcoholic. Not that Gigi had realised it when she was twelve years old. She had never seen her mother drinking, and her strong perfume was an attempt to hide the stench of alcohol. Viorica Alexa complained about Gigi's dad, that he was never around, that he never paid her any attention, that he didn't love her. Gigi's father had either ignored her or shouted at her, and both of them had been too wrapped up in themselves to worry about a child who had learnt very early on to fend for herself.

She had blamed herself for years for not being able to save her mother. She hated her father for driving Viorica to commit suicide. It was only when she grew up that she realised that her mother should have been looking after her, rather than the other way round. She had never even left her a note.

All this pain was the reason why Gigi had cut herself for several years in her teens. She had hardly ever cut her arms, she had preferred cutting her legs. She would take a sharp razor blade and cut very carefully, never allowing too much blood to flow. The pain was not immediate. She would watch the fine incision until the red drops started to appear. Sometimes she would touch them with her finger and then put the pain onto her tongue. That salty metallic taste. When she felt the pain in her leg, her heart felt lighter. The more immediate pain drove out the duller, more continuous one. At least for a while.

She shook off the painful memories and got up to make a coffee. She switched on her laptop. She searched for more details about Medea and read the script again, as well as the reviews. At least her mother had spared her the details, the drama. She simply took a fistful of sleeping pills rather than cutting her veins. She appreciated that now – cynical as she had become in her pain.

The reviewers talked about the couple's desperate search for happiness. For Gigi, it felt like the play was more about the dangers lurking in our minds when we fall in love. She herself knew from experience: the two years she had been with Vlad had taken her to the cliff edge, and it could all have ended far worse than it did. When he started stalking her, she got scared. How could love turn so quickly into hatred? And if he returned to Braşov, what would that be like? She realised she was still unclear how she felt about him now, still puzzled how she could have loved him so much at one time.

One particular passage from the play stuck in her head, when the man sees the woman in the park:

'I crossed over and followed her into the nearby park. She allowed herself to be followed. It was like going on a lion hunt without any weapons. I had to bring the lioness home, not kill her. The lioness sat down on a bench.'

On the poster, Andrada Vasiliu's traits had been slightly altered to resemble a predator. How ironic! The predator had become the prey.

She called the theatre in Târgu Mureş, where the original author of the play, Roxana Marian, was working. After being kept on hold for quite some time, she finally found her.

'Hello, I am Gigi Alexa, pathologist and collaborator with the police unit. I would like to ask you a few questions about your play Medea.'

'How come? I have to say, I find that surprising.'

'Let me explain. Andrada Vasiliu is an actress here in Braşov, who recently appeared in an independent production of your play. Do you know how she got hold of your text? Have you ever spoken to her directly?'

'Why are you calling me? I don't understand!'

'You might have missed it in the news. Andrada Vasiliu was killed a few days ago. We are investigating the murder, so any information about her could be useful.'

'I see. Well, I'm sorry, but I'm very surprised, that's all. Not that I don't want to help, but... Andrada called me two years ago asking for permission to perform the text. We didn't know each other, she found the play on a literature site. The play isn't currently being performed.'

'I was wondering if there was a particular reason why she wanted this play. Did she mention anything?'

'I just know she found Medea fascinating. She wanted to play that character and so she found my play. I had already adapted it as a one-woman show for Italy, so I simply sent her that text.'

'Did you see her perform it?'

'No. She did invite me to the premiere, but I couldn't go at the time. It wasn't performed that frequently, if I'm not mistaken. She had some kind of partnership with the Reduta Cultural Centre or something.'

'Do you know how many times it was performed? Andrada was killed after the performance on Sunday night.'

'I could check. She had offered me 10% of earnings for every performance, once she had paid off the venue and any other costs. Tiny sums, but I can check how often she deposited them into my account.'

'Don't worry, we can always ask the theatre. Do you have anything else to add? Anything you feel might be helpful?'

'It's probably not relevant, but when she called me to ask for permission, she told me she would have preferred a different ending. She insisted on it, in fact. That Medea had killed her children. I started telling her about the myth, that the infanticide appears to be pure invention on Euripides' part, that it was all about revenge and so on, but I could tell she wasn't listening. I got quite upset then.'

'And what happened? Did she ask you to make any changes?'

'No, she said she would perform the play as it was.'

'Did you keep in touch?'

'We spoke just once, after the premiere. She said it had gone well. That's all.'

'Thank you for being so open.'

'Does the crime have anything to do with the play?'

'I'm afraid I cannot answer that. I just wanted to get to know Andrada Vasiliu better, and I think what you told me perhaps deserves further exploration. Thank you so much, and if you do remember anything else here is my number.'

It seemed to be a dead end. The parents were too mild to be the source of Andrada's obsession with this play. Her father seemed timid, allowing himself to be guided by the mother. If there was any alcohol involved, it didn't seem to go as far as any abuse. It sounded like they would have to investigate the former lover, the one who said he hadn't been in touch with her since they split up.

'Good morning, Matei, were you still sleeping?'

'Of course not, it's ten!'

'Don't mind me and my silly jokes. Listen, what did the former lover say about Andrada? Why did they split up?'

'He said she wanted more commitment and he wasn't ready for it.'

'Can you give me his number?'

'I'll text it to you.'

She may not have woken up Matei, but she certainly did wake up Dragoş Apostol. He answered the phone very sleepily after she let it ring for a long while. Her questions surprised him but she found what she was looking for.

**

Matei, Marcel and Paul were standing beside her next to the two boards filled with pictures. They were asking the most absurd questions. After just a few minutes, they realised they had so few concrete questions to ask about the cases themselves that they had to dig a little deeper into alternative theories.

'What did Andrada's boyfriend say?'

'I asked him if she ever had an abortion. And it appears that she did indeed get rid of a pregnancy just as they were breaking up. It really upset her. She was pregnant with twins.'

'So they didn't question him very deeply,' said Matei. 'Although I'm not sure how this piece of information helps us any further.'

'I'm not sure either. But it just shows she was very impressionable, hurt and vulnerable. That's why she was so interested in Medea. There is even a medical syndrome with that name, a derivative of the Munchausen syndrome, in which a mother kills her babies. But I don't know if that is a solid theory. Paul, did you manage to get into her account?'

'Yes, but I haven't found anything relevant. She only had conversations with the people she knew, she never bothered to reply to admirers or trolls.'

'So zilch there,' Matei slammed the papers onto the table. 'Anything in the Irina Oprea case?'

'She did reply to various guys online, but nothing out of the ordinary. Just a few horny messages, you know, sexting, that kind of thing.'

'Did she meet any of them?'

'I don't think so. Or if they did, they stopped texting.'

'How did you get into their Facebook account though? Wasn't there some password?' asked Gigi.

'Via the phone. Once I managed to log into the phone, I just logged onto the app automatically.'

'That simple?'

'Not always, so don't worry too much about it.'

'I have no intention of using social media, no problem. There's only one reality, why should we create an alternative one...'

She moved closer to the board and pointed at one of the pictures of the braids that had been cut off and the ponytail that was in the bin.

'Why not take the hair if he cut it off? That's what I don't understand.'

'What do you mean?'

'Cutting hair off is like a trophy. Hair represents power, see Samson and Delilah, so cutting off someone's hair means you punish or shame them. Since he threw it in the bin, this feels more like a shaming act, or else he is punishing her for something that she has done or something that she is. Maybe he did keep at least one braid back for himself. Has anyone checked?'

'You're asking me?' Matei shook his head. 'How could you even tell? There are so many braids. He could easily have taken one.'

'We could tell. We count how many were cut off and how many are left on the head. There is a risk that they were of different lengths, but it's worth a try. I will ask Mr Ispas to do the job. He'll complain, but needs must. So, if one of them is missing, then we might be able to link the two cases, and he would have taken the braid as a trophy.'

'You think so? Seems a bit far-fetched to me. He did take the cash register after all.'

'That was just to make us think that it was a robbery. Which might mean he is planning something else. I'm finding it very tricky to link the two cases. We might be wasting a lot of time trying to find a connection. I simply cannot get a handle on this kind of perpetrator. With a serial killer, they usually start slowly and then escalate. But here we have two cases within the space of a couple of days, and both done very rapidly. I can't detect a pattern.'

'Ok, we'll leave you to it.'

'In fact, I might go and count the braids myself. I think we're done for the day. Aren't you?'

'I'll start typing up the report.' Matei accompanied her down the corridor. 'I wanted to let you know that Tomescu is here.'

'Hmm. Can't be helped!' Gigi sighed. 'We'll manage

somehow Have you found out if he's here on official business about our cases, or is there something else?'

'I just saw him briefly at lunchtime. He said he is just checking up on things, doesn't want to interfere, blah blah. But I think we both know that's not the reason he's here.'

'Stop with your innuendos! There's no way he is here for me.'

'I just like to tease you...'

'Have a nice evening. I'll call you if there's anything to report.'

**

The days were getting shorter. Barely perceptible as yet, but there was this sensation of darkness looming. Especially when she compared it with midsummer, when it was always light outside when she left the morgue. Except for the days when Radu would take her out in the evening right after work. She didn't quite know if she liked that or found it slightly annoying. Tomorrow he would be back and would want to spend more time with her. Their relationship had lasted a whole year, which was unusual for her. She had never been in a long-term relationship before, nor lived with an unrelated someone in the same house. It was no big deal for ordinary people, but she seldom went by what others did.

Her phone vibrated in her pocket.

'Ah, Matei, sorry I forgot to call. I spoke to Ispas.'

'I was curious, even though it's probably nothing.'

'Indeed There were 45 braids on her head, and 45 were found in the bin.'

'Her son has shown up. He's outside.'

'Poor man.'

'Can he come and see you tomorrow morning? When will you be finished with her?'

'Lemnaru will check and counter-sign the day after

tomorrow, I believe. That's when they can pick up the body. But if he wants to talk to me beforehand, I can see him tomorrow.'

'He'll call you before coming in. I'll give him your number.'

'Great. I'll be there at eight. Unless something else happens.'

'Is that a smile I hear in your voice?'

'Not at all. Good night!'

**

Gigi could feel a strong scent as soon as she entered the hallway. There was no one in the dining room. The scent was familiar, but she couldn't quite place it. She heard a noise.

'Morty, is that you? Did you just demolish something? Morty?'

The cat came up to her, meowing and curling around her legs. She bent down and picked him up, rubbed her forehead against his and then put him down, as he started protesting.

'Yes, you crosspatch! All you want is a short cuddle and then you're off.'

She opened the door to the living room. The odour was stronger here. By the time she got to the bedroom, she remembered: *Allure* by Dior. Her hand went straight to her throat and she tried to turn back. He couldn't have got in. He wouldn't have hidden out in the bathroom. It must be someone else. She checked her pocket for her phone. Her earbuds were in, as usual, she pressed the record button and said: 'Aha!' to start recording. She stepped forward, took a deep breath and pushed heavily against the bathroom door. Radu dropped the showerhead and started yelling.

She tried to recover her composure. 'Darling, I wanted to surprise you, I realised you had come back.' She walked up to him to kiss him.

'You'll get wet. I ll be right out. I thought I would be the one to surprise you.'

'Why did you return earlier?'

'I got bored,' Radu smiled.

'Sure, Amsterdam is a notoriously boring place. Were you worried about me?'

'A little bit.'

'Fine, I'll leave you to it. I'll try and fix something to eat. Probably a salad, since I wasn't expecting you until tomorrow, so there isn't much in the fridge.'

'I brought a few things from the duty free. Some caviar, two types of cheese and foie gras. Acceptable?'

'I'll see if I have any bread that isn't mouldy. Hurry up.'

She found a lot of parcels waiting to be opened on the kitchen table. She started unpacking, but there was no mistaking the smell of the camembert. She took a deep breath and decided to make a salad to go with that. She was surprised by the three bottles of wine. A brand she was unfamiliar with, but she thought the minimalist label with a horse's skull, white on a burgundy background, was quite striking. *Dark Horses*, it was called, a Cabernet Sauvignon – interesting choice. She struggled to open one of the bottles, to let the wine breathe, and put the remaining two away in the cupboard.

**

She was back in the bathroom, alone this time. Radu was setting the table and she was sitting on the toilet lid, while the shower was running. Living together meant that you had to steal occasional moments to be by yourself.

After they had made love, Radu had another shower and showed her the new perfume he had bought at the duty free. The same one that Vlad used. That was why she panicked when she walked into the house. She was over-tired, clearly.

8

The Fourth

The night was unusually warm. Summer's last stand, perhaps. The road to the stud farm was empty. He left the car at the edge of town and ran the rest of the way, to avoid being spotted. He was dressed in black top to toe and kept away from the main road, even though there was no way they could identify him. Even his shoes were black.

When he reached the stables, he slid to the edge of the perimeter. The CCTV cameras were focused on the main road. The horses were quiet, although some of them let out a soft snort as he passed by. His footsteps were completely silent. He walked to the end of the stables then went back outside. No sign of any guard, he'd have to find him first.

He went back in and switched on the torch on his mobile, rather than relying on the dim light inside the stables. He heard a faint sound and managed to identify where it came from. It was the snoring of the man who was supposed to look after this place, probably drunk. He smiled when he found him asleep on the straw in the last stall. He bent over him, pushed him with his toe, but the drunk man didn't react. He was about to leave him alone, but then changed his mind and came back. The man didn't even shudder when he stuck the syringe into his shoulder to sedate him further.

He struggled a bit with the fire hydrant, but finally

managed to open it, as well as the other tap at the entrance to the stables. Then he closed the door and disappeared into the darkness.

9

It was a frustrating weekend. Gigi would almost have preferred not to have him back. When there wasn't much going on at work, or nothing urgent, she was happy to spend time with him, but when she was busy, when she had a lot to read and think about, Radu just wore her out. She would have liked to be able to tell him that she needed more space, but she was mindful of hurting him. The entire weekend he had wanted something from her – to go into town, to dine together by candlelight or at a restaurant in the centre. Then, on Sunday afternoon, he was called in for an emergency and she did her best to mask her relief.

She had been reading for an hour when he finally showed signs of waking up.

'Morning, did you manage to get any rest? What time did you get back?'

'Morning, my love. I think it was two in the morning. It was awful.'

'Did something go wrong?'

'In the end, it didn't, but I had to stay because Blanche, the prize mare, started her contractions too early.'

'Is the foal OK?'

'Yes, he's fine. I was worried, because she was supposed to give birth in two weeks' time, but apparently she had a bit of a shock.'

'Why, what happened?'

'We don't know. The stable hand was so drunk that you

couldn't understand a word he said. He was fast asleep. We don't know if he turned on the taps, including the fire hydrant, and then forgot about them and fell asleep. He was soaked, I think he only woke up when he was about to drown. He was lucky, in any case, some people were going up that route to get to a B&B and they saw water pouring out into the road. They called 112, the security company called the owners and they called us. I'm sorry I had to leave you alone most of Sunday.'

'No worries.'

'It was my day off, but Marian couldn't handle it all on his own. They thought something might have happened to the horses, but it wasn't anything too serious.'

'What a stupid waste though! How much water was there?'

'Quite a bit, as you can imagine, if it flowed out into the road. The people who called it in thought that a pipe had burst.'

'And you think the stable hand did this?'

'Not sure. He didn't look too good, hope he gets over it. He was completely blotto. Can you imagine, sitting in that cold water and not being able to get up or raise the alarm? At the very least, I'd say he'll get pneumonia. The owners said they might take him to court. Anyway, they're facing a huge bill. They might be insured and recover some of the money. But there must be better methods to clean up the place.'

'Why are you smiling?'

'Because they really cleaned the place like I've seldom seen before. By the time we left, there was fresh straw everywhere, it was all sparkling fresh. I'll go and bring you coffee, you stay in bed.'

'Thanks. Are you off to the practice?'

'Yes, I'm on early shift this week. You?'

'I have to go to the police. We're back at square one.'

'I'm sorry.'

'Why?'

'To see you struggling so hard.'

'There's something else. Which might explain why I'm so out of sorts. Tomescu is back.'

'Since when?'

'Last week. But I haven't seen him yet. Today's the day.' Gigi grimaced.

'Do you want me to pick you up?'

'No, I'll be fine. But I'm in no mood to see him.'

'Gigi, it's been a while...'

'I know. There's nothing there. But I do wish he hadn't come back.'

'Why, is he planning to take his old job back?'

'I hope not. Although Matei did say he had some trouble in Bucharest and they might want to get rid of him. I doubt it's anything permanent though, and I don't think he really wants to be here.'

'You're afraid he'll pester you?'

'I'm not afraid, I just have this unpleasant feeling.'

**

Gigi was tempted to put on dark clothes, maybe black, which was highly unusual for her. She usually preferred bright colours, the wilder the better. She hadn't worn black since the Fora case. Black, for her, meant fear, she realised. While lying in hospital after the attack, she had asked Matei to bring her black clothes from home, which she kept in a separate section of her wardrobe.

Black was danger and, for a moment there, she had believed that Vlad might have attempted to poison her. When she confessed that, Vlad had been very hurt. He found it difficult to accept that she could have seen a cold-blooded killer in him.

She finally chose a striped outfit, purple and green, as lively as possible, to make up for the death she was constantly surrounded with at work. For most people, death was the furthest thing from their mind. She could see that when they came to the morgue. They had that one brief moment of being confronted with the transience of life, but they generally tried to avoid dealing with the fact that humans were in fact such a fragile species. They went back to their lives, hungry for petty objects and ambitions, without reflecting at all upon the essence of life.

**

Irina Oprea's son had been very stoic. She had received him on Friday morning and taken him first to her office, where she made him a coffee. He had asked details about his mother's death, whether she had suffered. She spared him any gruesome details, didn't even mention the hair being cut off. But she didn't lie to him either, she said that his mother must have been frightened. His eyes were swivelling, staring all around the office, before he finally sat down on the red leather sofa. He had been close to tears, but then his eyes fell on the black and white drawings she had on the walls.

'Are those portraits of you?'

They were indeed very expressive, one in profile and one frontal. A painter and illustrator who had been in love with her for about three months a long time ago.

Looking more closely, she was certain that the thin line on her neck in one of the portraits hadn't been there before. She instinctively lifted her hand to her neck, as if there was a burning sensation cutting across her skin. Then she told herself she must be going crazy. It must have been there for a while, things like that don't happen overnight. The drawings had been hanging in her office for so long that she hadn't examined them closely in ages.

'Thank you for speaking to me,' he said at last.

'It must be so hard for you.'

'Yes, we were very close, in spirit, if not geographically...'

A tear slid down his cheek. Tudor took a tissue from the box on the coffee table and wiped it away.

'Are you married, Tudor?'

'No. I have a girlfriend, we live together in Verona.'

'Very nice. Verona, I mean. Is she here with you?'

'No. I knew it might take a while so I told her to stay there until it was all over. Will it take much longer?'

'We should be ready by next week and you can pick her up. Do you have any other relatives?'

'No. My dad went off to Spain in 2008 and we haven't heard from him since. He wasn't living with us anyway, my mother raised me all by herself. Her sisters are both in Italy as well, in Sicily. I told them to come here later, for the funeral. They are much older than my mother, one is over sixty, the other nearing seventy. It's hard, Dr Alexa. In Italy, I look after ladies who are older than them. Do you know any undertakers, by any chance?'

'Of course. There's a list in the entrance hall, all vetted by us.'

'Thank you.'

'Tudor, if you don't mind me asking, was your mother seeing anyone?'

'I'm not sure. She had a boyfriend until last year, but nothing after that. She would visit my aunts every now and then, stay for a bit, even work a little out there. Why, do you think it was someone she knew?'

'Just checking. Do you happen to know when she had her braids done?'

'This summer, when she visited Aunt Doina in Catania. An African lady did it for her. About a month ago.'

'Thank you. If you remember anything else, please call me or else Chief Inspector Vălean.'

The death of a parent is usually the first time we confront mortality. It is far easier to ignore the unknown or secondary people who disappear from our lives, they come and go, there is no way they can be expected to last forever. But our mother has always been there, since the moment we were born, the first continuous presence in our life.

It was only when Gigi saw Viorica lying in the coffin that she realised her mum would never return. Her father was a bit scared about being a single father, but also somewhat relieved. He was now rid of the nervous breakdowns of a woman who had been equally dependent on alcohol and on him and their toxic relationship. Now he was left with a twelve-year-old who considered him her mortal enemy. Gigi was used to being ignored and alone, but at least she had had Viorica to look after. Now the only thing left to fuel her was the hatred for her father.

This was most certainly not the case with Tudor Oprea: he was well-adjusted, mature, independent, he had a girlfriend. He would be fine, but she still pitied him with all her heart.

**

In the end she chose a blue dress over skinny jeans and a leather jacket, which she ended up carrying around for nothing all day. Radu was waiting for her in the car.

'What are you doing afterwards? When do you finish today?'

'I have no idea how long the police thing will last. And then I have to go to work. I was supposed to be doing the morning shift today, but Lemnaru allowed me to go in later.'

'Then are we meeting up at home at four?'

'Can't tell you. If we have a lot of work, I'll have to stay late to finish it. Emil is back from his annual leave today, but there's lots of stuff he needs to be updated on. Why, you worried?'

'A little '

'About Tomescu?'

'I think so,' Radu attempted a smile.

'Relax, he can't hurt me anymore.' She kissed Radu before getting out of the car in the police station parking lot.

The first person she encountered was none other than Vlad Tomescu. She first spotted his shoes, his favourite make, with pointed toes, veering dangerously close to winklepickers, even shinier than usual, not a speck of dust on them. Incredible for a city full of pollution, within spitting distance of the building site for the new commercial centre. He must have given them a wipe before stepping out of his car. He probably had a sponge in the glove compartment for no other purpose than that. His trousers were brown chinos without the tiniest crease, and the belt was shiny black leather, a bit of a showstopper. An immaculate white shirt. He was holding his navy-blue blazer casually slung over one shoulder, the laptop bag over the other. She put her hand to her chest when she caught his eye and coughed.

'Good morning, Gigi, I'm happy to see you again.'

'Morning, Vlad.'

'You couldn't say "likewise" if it killed you, could you?'

'How right you are, Vlad.'

'We should grab a coffee, don't you think?'

'Between friends, you mean?'

'We haven't seen each other in over a year. Maybe even eighteen months.'

'Maybe after the meeting.'

'I'd like that. Are you ill? You're coughing.'

'Maybe. I don't know.'

They entered the building together, and she continued straight up the stairs, while he stopped to greet people, shake hands with those who decided it might be better to suck up to their former boss once more, just in case he came back.

The meeting room had been set up for the briefing. Matei

was busy connecting the laptop to the projector on the table at the front of the room. Marcel came up to Gigi.

'Have you heard? The police chief will be here too.'

'I know I met him outside. He's busy being adored by the crowds, so it will take him a while to get here. There seem to be quite a few of us today.'

'Everyone working on each of the two cases.'

'Anything new come up?'

'Not much.' Marcel indicated the door opening and Vlad coming in with three other colleagues. 'Let's sit down.'

Gigi selected a seat in the second row, at the very edge. She might have collaborated on the Fora case, but she still felt like an outsider. She had been given an official title, but since there had been no other cases requiring her expertise, she considered it best to keep her counsel. She knew that quite a few of the people gathered here cast an unfavourable eye on her involvement, but without her they would never have solved the Fora case. She had to admit that even now she was unclear about Fora's motivation. A psychiatrist is of course surrounded by so much mental illness that it might escape his notice that he is suffering from something himself, but had there been anything else driving him, beyond his giant ego and desire to prove that anyone was capable of murder?

The first picture up on screen was of Andrada Vasiliu as she appeared on the morning they found her. Matei Vălean started off with a brief recap.

'If I may remind you, Andrada Vasiliu, actress at the theatre here in Braşov, had a show at the Reduta Centre the evening of the 2nd of September. After the show, she had something to drink with her colleagues on the terrace of the Gott Restaurant, and set off for home on her own at around 00:30. She was attacked on Vrancei Street, where she had been living on her own since her parents retired to the countryside. She was sedated with chloroform at the gate and taken inside the yard, where she was strangled, undressed, and had a fingernail pulled out. We found her clothes in the nearby woods afterwards. Her former lover, Dragoş Apostol, you can see his picture here, said that he had returned from Greece on the very morning her body was found. However, we discovered he entered the country the evening before, at 18:00. We will call him in for an official statement and see where he spent the intervening hours. Anything to add, Gigi?'

'Good morning, everyone, I just wanted to say that we don't need to worry too much about him. You should, however, check with his current girlfriend, who will probably confirm his alibi. Question: did you find out about anyone recently released from prison?'

'Not much movement in this area.'

'I just want us to avoid jumping to conclusions,' Gigi stood up and walked to the front of the room, in front of the screen. 'If it's not someone close to the victim, then we are in trouble. Because it will be far harder to establish a motive, or whatever you choose to call it. It's clear that Andrada Vasiliu was being stalked, that it was all premeditated, and that there is a relevant reason for this, at least in the killer's mind. Pulling out a fingernail looks like he was keeping a trophy from the victim.'

After finishing her speech, Gigi went back to her place.

'Any other questions?' Matei asked.

'Who spoke to the neighbours?' Tomescu asked, without getting up.

'I did,' said Marcel, standing up.

'Anything interesting there?'

'No one saw anything.'

'Something else I'm after. Any neighbour who got entangled with Andrada Vasiliu?'

'Nobody admitted to anything like that.'

'As if they would, unprompted. Aren't there any little old ladies living on that street?' asked Tomescu.

'There are some a little further down, in the older houses.'

'Those are the people you should be speaking to. They've got nothing better to do than to watch and find out everything that is happening behind closed doors. If it's someone who lives in the area, that would explain why there were no suspicious people caught on camera. The perpetrator must have walked down that road several times to be able to attack her so accurately, so efficiently. He knew the territory. You have to ask the little old ladies if they saw any strangers in the area.'

'I did ask them that.'

'You personally or your PCs?'

'The PCs,' Marcel lowered his head.

'Anyway, I want to congratulate the Chief Inspector and the entire team for all your hard work over the weekend. Shall we move onto the next case?'

There was a hurried knock at the door and Nicu Mocanu rushed into the room.

'Sorry to interrupt, but can someone please come downstairs to calm down a gentleman who has come to give a statement but insists he will only speak to a senior officer?'

'What's it about?'

'He says he was pushed and fell on the Postăvaru last Thursday, and he wants us to search for the man who did it. He gave a statement in hospital but no one has been in touch with him since, or so he says. He's being quite... aggressive.'

'Does he have a description of the man?' Matei switched off the projector and headed towards the door.

'That's the issue: he says he didn't get to see him. We've tried to reason with him.'

'Marcel, can I ask you to go, please?' Tomescu interrupted, eager to solve the situation quickly.

Marcel stood up slowly, looking at his commanding officer, Matei, to see if he agreed. Tomescu looked away.

'Yes, fine, Marcel, please go and take his statement.

We'll continue here. Right, moving on to Irina Oprea,' said Matei, switching the projector on again. 'The hairdressing salon is on Calea Bucureşti, entrance directly on the main road. A block of flats has recently been built behind it and therefore there've been numerous power cuts recently, something the neighbours confirmed. I asked for a detailed report from the energy provider, but it might take some time. They panicked a little when the police contacted them. Oprea's colleagues, her friends and her son all say that they were unaware of any serious relationship in the last few months. The big question here is whether this one was premeditated or not. Even if it was just a robbery. Was someone staking out the place and waiting for a power cut? Or was it someone who happened to be walking down the street, and took advantage of the sudden darkness? Yes, Gigi? You wanted to say something?'

'Judging by the actions there, I would say once again that this was personal. Irina Oprea was the target, not the robbery. I can see you looking puzzled. Well, this cutting of the hair is somewhat symbolic: punishment, shaming, we will know exactly what when we get closer to our perpetrator. But it's no coincidence. I think the power cut was simply a bonus for him, but he would have done it anyway. Even if it hadn't been dark.'

'But then why did he take the money? Can you explain that?' Matei raised his voice a little.

'He might have actually needed the money, or else he was trying to mislead us. I don't like the second option at all.'

'Why not?' Tomescu seemed genuinely curious.

'Because it means he's playing for time. Which means he is planning something more. OK, he might not have taken a braid as a trophy, but he may have taken something else. Maybe the money box itself is a trophy, although it doesn't feel like a personal object belonging to the victim. But I don't think it was a plain old robbery.'

'Can you give us a portrait of the killer?'

'Only that it's a man of around 30-50, relatively intelligent, even if not necessarily formally educated. I don't know if we should dig any deeper in her list of acquaintances.'

'I suggest we first ask all those with whom she chatted online or on her phone. Paul, please make a list of those men and any details about what they discussed and give it to Marcel to distribute to everyone who is working on the case,' said Matei, walking up to the pictures of the two cases. 'Gigi, can you tell us if you think the two cases are related?'

She stood up and joined Matei beside the two boards.

'It would be very serious if that were indeed the case. What are we talking about here? A man who expresses two entirely different things with each of the two crimes. In the first case, the victim is undressed and placed in a sphinx-like position – although we could also call it a subservient position. In the second case, her head is on the table and her hair is in the rubbish bin. Each of this must mean something, but I cannot see a connection between them, aside from perhaps a general contempt for women. If it is the same perpetrator, all I can say is that something else will follow. But he is holding back, he's not given us enough information yet.'

'That sounds very sinister!' Tomescu joined them at the front of the room.

'I know. I suggest we continue investigating the two cases separately, but also keep an open mind to the fact that they might be linked.'

The heavy silence that followed was interrupted by Marcel tiptoeing back into the room.

'Well, if there is nothing else to discuss, then off to work. Paul, make a list of each contact, when they called, any messages, and so on for each of the two cases. Please check everything. We don't really know what we are looking for.

We want to see if any of the people surrounding the victims started behaving strangely at any point. Thank you all, you're free to go.'

Matei made a big deal about packing up his laptop and said to Gigi in a low tone, 'Can you see me in my office?'

'Right now?'

'Yes.'

'Gigi, can I ask you something?' Tomescu planted himself in front of her as she tried to leave the room.

'Sure.'

'I have more questions about the case, but not here.'

'Where, then?'

'Over a coffee?'

'Do we have to?'

'Please. It would be strictly about the cases, I promise.'

'So I can't refuse, can I?'

'Glad to see you understand me. I'll be waiting for you on the third floor, I've got an office there, first door on the left.'

'Fine, I'll be there after I've spoken to Matei.'

**

Matei had changed the office décor since he took over from Vlad. He had taken out the giant brown leather sofa and replaced it with a far smaller, more modest two-seater in grey linen and a round table with four comfortable chairs, very much like armchairs. On the wall he had a map of Brașov. He had stuck a little flag on the Vrancei Street in the Șchei and another on Calea București.

'Gigi, do you realise what it means if the cases are linked?'

'Of course. That's why I'm reluctant to jump to conclusions.'

'What could the motive be?'

'If they are linked, the motive might be humiliating

these women. Taking off their clothes or their hair, those are powerful symbols, at least in his vision. Don't forget he discarded Andrada's clothes in the forest. It would be a hell of a coincidence if the two women, who otherwise didn't have anything in common, were involved at any point with the same man, with someone capable of doing such a thing. I mean, it's not impossible. But there is a greater probability, and that is far worse, that the victims were chosen for what they represent to him, not because they had a relationship with him.'

'What about the option that they each had a relationship with a different individual who had issues?'

'Highly improbable. In fact, the more I think about it, the less I believe it. There are too many similarities between the two cases for it to be a simple coincidence.'

She jumped when Matei slammed his coffee cup on the glass top table.

'No need to get upset, Matei. I merely say that so we can be prepared if anything else comes along. What is the press saying?'

'Think I have time for them?'

'Well, you should. It will get messy very soon. Have you prepared a statement? Talk with Alina about it.'

'She's working on something now. Do you think we should do a press conference?'

'Not yet. But if we do decide the cases are linked, we absolutely must. Simple option would be that they both knew the same person, otherwise... the more frightening option is that the killer had no direct connection to them. In that case, we are fucked!'

'Thanks for the reassurance.'

'I'm sorry.' Gigi rose and put a hand on his shoulder. 'Really, it's complicated. I've got to go see Tomescu.'

'Going out with him?'

'No, going to his office. Can you keep me informed if you hear that Tomescu is planning to move back here?'

'Of course.'

Just as she was about to go out the door, Matei caught up with her.

'Can you give me a hug? I feel we are in deep shit now.'

Gigi laughed as she hugged him.

**

Vlad always accused her of being malicious and unforgiving; and of blaming him for things he had never even considered doing. But the horrendous way in which he had harassed her after they broke up had left deep scars within her. She entered his office with a heavy heart.

'Hello again, Vlad.'

'Please come in. Look, I've even made coffee.'

'What did you want to see me about?'

'I wanted to hear what you feel about all of this. Not the facts, not what you can prove, but your gut feeling.'

She walked up to the window and repeated the arguments she had already discussed with Matei.

'But which option do you think it is? What does your intuition tell you?'

'Intuition is something related to a logic that we simply cannot quite perceive yet. I think this story has a pattern that we don't quite get yet.'

'So the victims are chosen randomly?'

'No, not that. Rather, they are chosen according to some criteria that we are incapable of perceiving just yet. But the perpetrator does.'

'So you do think it's the same person?'

'Yes, but I don't think he knew them. Or at least he wasn't close to either of them.'

'That's worse.'

'I know. And I don't have a clue how to tackle this.'

He took both coffee cups from the table and brought them up to the window, handing one to Gigi.

'Drink it before it gets cold.'

She took the coffee cup from him, making a great effort not to touch his hand. Then she turned to look outside again.

'What's that monstrosity they're building there? When will it be done?' Vlad tried to make small talk.

'May next year, or so they say.'

'What a horror! A shopping mall in the centre of town. It will be dire. There won't be any more traffic on this road.'

'It's bad enough already. Did you see that giant hole they dug? It looks like an enormous grave.' Gigi laughed.

'You and your morbid imagination! Have you decided what you want to do in the future? Staying with the department?'

'Vlad, this whole collaboration is a bit of misnomer. I'm an occasional consultant, nothing more. The only difference is that now I have an official badge to be nosy, but in fact nothing much has changed. I've simply raised a few hackles. A lot of people have insinuated you did me this favour so that you could get rid of me. Or it was you finding a way to pay me. True, that is the difference now – I'm getting paid for my consultancy work.'

'Just let them be, there will always be haters.'

'Probably. Anyway, I want to start a Ph.D. in the Netherlands on victimology.'

'Great, when do you start?'

'I've probably missed the deadline for this year, because I would need to be in Groningen between the 20th and 30th of September to have an interview. I sent them all the paperwork, but they want to meet me in person.'

'And what makes you think you won't be able to go?'

'Because I don't know what will happen here. I don't know why, but I have the feeling this is just the beginning.'

'Maybe it won't be that bad.' Vlad paused then took another step forward towards the window. Gigi measured the space between them and stepped sideways.

'Please don't come any closer.'

'I didn't mean anything... are you all right?'

'I think so, yes. But I would have liked to know that you regret what happened and how much you hurt me.'

'Can we just leave the past behind? No point in flogging to death something that no longer exists...'

'I no longer feel that acute pain, true enough, but something changed in me after you did what you did. I felt in real danger. I thought you wanted to kill me.'

'And I told you at the time that it was just your imagination. I was hurt too that you could believe that about me. Seriously, can we just let the past go?'

'How strange – I still held a faint hope that you could behave responsibly and take your share of the blame for what happened back then. Have I ever told you I wanted to kill my father?'

'What?'

'I couldn't get over my mother's death. I held him responsible for it. We were in Greece together and I prepared oleander tea for him. I'm not sure it would have been deadly, but what's important is that I thought that only by killing him could I avenge Mum's death.'

'Your overactive brain again...'

'You find it hard to accept that people can admit their flaws and mistakes. Naturally, because you never admit your own.'

'You've always misjudged me. Your opinion has to prevail. But things are far more complicated than that...'

'Let me finish my story. I threw the tea away after my father begged me for forgiveness. He told me how sorry he was for all the bad things he had done to my mother, and I believed him. I think that's what I was hoping to hear from you. That you are sorry.' Gigi set her coffee cup on the windowsill and looked him straight in the eye. 'And now we had better each go our separate way.'

'I'm glad we're able to set the past to one side.'

'Of course you are. Are you moving back to Braşov?'

'Not sure. I might be seconded here for a while. I am a nuisance in Bucharest.'

'You, who are so good at charming people?'

'Alas, there are two camps in Bucharest: the ones who try to act with integrity and the ones who try to hide any mistakes or systemic failures. I'm referring to the Caracal case, of course. I fell into the first camp, I even wrote up a report pointing out all the shortcomings in the way that case was handled. And I lost. The head of the service resigned, the police chief was fired. And that was about the extent of it.'

**

During her conversation with Vlad, Gigi had managed to keep a neutral tone, to protect herself from any show of emotion. She had wrapped herself up in a cocoon, to keep a safe distance from everything and everyone. She left the police station via the barrier, the access route for the general public. She walked past those waiting in the hallways almost as if they were immovable objects, trying to stay away from anything they said or did. She looked on the other side of the road, where other people, other cars seemed so distant. She shook her head, trying to recover. She could never quite explain to Vlad how scared she had been back then, how much it had hurt her to think he could ever wish to harm her.

When her father died, she had gone through a difficult period at university. She might have intended to poison him at one time, but once he had admitted his sincere regrets, their relationship had improved. Many of her friends and acquaintances had showed up at his funeral in Frankfurt, where he had been living with Elfriede for nearly a year. But when she returned to Romania, she couldn't help feeling that she was all alone in the world. It was the hardest summer of her life. She had no idea how the days passed until she started her second year at university.

When her course started on the 1st of October, she'd felt a more positive energy. She wanted to get to know her fellow students, show more interest in them and their hobbies. She started going to parties, then realised that she was a little in love with a certain young man in her year. He seemed to be the coolest guy in their year, good-looking, with long hair. He was very much aware that all the girls fancied him, so he made zero effort to approach any of them, waiting for them to make the first step. Maybe what he liked about Gigi was that she was too shy to attempt to seduce him with cigarettes or cakes, like the other girls did.

She had moved out of student halls into a small studio flat in Mănăştur, and she enjoyed living among normal people. Auntie Mimi who lived opposite, for example, was very kind, a little intrusive to start with, until Gigi realised she was only trying to help. She had two young boys and kept calling her 'Doctor'.

She was late to the party that night because one of Mimi's boys had suddenly developed a high fever and she had stayed with him until his temperature went down. The rooms in the student hall were full of smoke. Everyone was reasonably drunk by the time she arrived. They were singing and dancing to a lively beat and burst out in cheers when they saw her. The cool guy walked up to her, kissed her on the cheek and started twirling her around. She hugged him and laughed. She drank whatever they offered her: wine, beer, sour cherry liqueur. As they danced a slow dance, her body was close to Bogdan's, or Boby, as everyone called him. Her head was on his shoulder, and she could feel the warmth of his hands stroking her body.

'I'm sleepy,' she whispered in Boby's ear.

She could feel him smiling as he held her even more tightly.

'We could go to my room, you could sleep there. It's three in the morning, no point going home at this time of night.'

They walked down the corridor tightly entwined, tripping a little on the stairs and laughing. When they got to his room, Gigi was surprised to discover there were only two beds.

'There are only two of you here?'

'Yes, we bought out the other two places, so it's a bit like sharing a studio, minus the kitchen.'

She lay down on the bed and covered herself with the blanket. The walls seemed to be moving in and out in slow motion, and she fell asleep as if she were being rocked in a cradle. She woke up suddenly, dreaming she was being suffocated. It was Boby on top of her, he had pinned her arms above her head with his hands. Her blouse was pulled up to her neck and he was struggling to pull down her trousers.

'What are you doing, Boby? Let me go! I can't breathe.'

'I'm doing what I've wanted to do from the moment you walked in through that door tonight. And I know you want it too.'

'No, I don't, Bogdan. Leave me alone! Get off!'

'Be quiet! Don't bother struggling!'

'Stop, Bogdan. I'll scream!'

He got off the bed at an angle, her knee couldn't reach to kick him. He sat on the bed and slapped her so hard that her head hit the wall. She thought she could feel blood in her mouth, but it was tears, equally salty but less viscous.

He took her blouse and stuffed it in her mouth. He told her that no one could hear her. She stopped trying to scream. Not even when he pulled down her trousers and underwear. Not even when he entered her with a sudden painful push. The pain between her legs was just the final piece of the puzzle, but above all there was the pain of the emptiness inside her.

She pushed him away after he fell asleep on top of her. She got up and went to the bathroom, where she threw up several times. She sat on the toilet and counted the white square tiles on the wall; at least ten of them were chipped.

Finally, she stood up and got into the shower. She deliberately chose to handle it all by herself, as always. She could have gone to the police, but her blood alcohol levels were high and she had gone willingly to his room. They would have asked her what she thought would happen when she agreed to go to his room. They would have said that others had seen his hands wandering all over her body while dancing, that he had even squeezed her breast and she had let him do it.

What could she say? That it wasn't true? They had all witnessed it at the party. That she had changed her mind once she had gone to his room and got into his bed? No, it was all too humiliating.

The water was evaporating on her body, chilling her to the core. She sniffed at the two towels hanging on the hook and picked the drier one. Maybe Bogdan had taken a shower before going to the party. She wrapped the towel around her and went back to the room. He had turned to the wall and was snoring. Her trousers were on the floor. She bent over to pick them up and her towel slid off. She found her underwear under his jeans, and she started to shiver. It was anger, she knew that. Her blouse was somewhere in the bed, under his body. She decided to leave it there and find something else in the wardrobe.

After she got dressed, she looked at him sleeping. It was still dark, only a faint light came from outside, bathing the room in a blue and golden-red haze. Her first thought was to shave his head. Her second was to stick a knife into him. But, in both cases, there was a strong possibility he might wake up. Bogdan was strong, her jaw still hurt from the slap he had given her. It was too risky to wake him up, to have him retaliate.

Her short-term solution would have been to kill him. But in the long-term...

It didn't take long to make up her mind. She got up and left through the empty corridors. There was still music pounding from the upper floor, where the party had been. She could have gone to pick up her jacket, but she couldn't face the others. They might be too drunk to notice her, but she was suddenly too cold and ran away.

When she got home, she jumped into the shower once more, letting the water get hotter and hotter, even hotter than her tears, which flowed down her cheeks until she could no longer feel them. The next day she went to buy the morning-after pill.

She had never told anyone about this. Mimi asked her a couple of times if she was all right but didn't insist. For a few months she wore only black, as if in mourning, but after that she decided never to wear that colour again.

When Vlad had started stalking her during the Fora case, all that fear and powerlessness had resurfaced. It was like the cells in her body had suddenly recovered the memory of the rape. Of course, Vlad did not know why she had reacted like that, and she had no intention of telling him.

**

She took off her coat and stuffed it into her bag. Her earbuds slipped out and got entangled in her hair, so she took them off and dropped them into her bag as well. The military unit on Titulescu Street was being refurbished. A few soldiers were outside, two of them plastering with trowels, the others just watching them. Not surprising, this lack of efficiency. At this rate, they might finish repainting the whole thing in two months, although it shouldn't take them longer than a week.

Gigi's phone rang and she had to put her bag down, take out her coat, then her folder with reports and photos, then her wallet, a bag for life which she always kept in her bag just in case, and finally her phone. Radu.

'How are you, my beauty? Shall I reserve a table for us somewhere, for tonight?'

'Are we celebrating something?'

'Yes, my return, isn't that reason enough?'

'Radu, I'm not sure when I'll be finished here. I should have gone in this morning...'

'I thought you'd be glad.'

'I'm going through a difficult period right now, please understand.'

'Fine, I'll stop bothering you.'

'That sounds a bit passive-aggressive, if I'm not mistaken.'

'All you do is criticise me...'

'And all you do is take offence.'

'Fine. Bye!'

'Radu! Radu?'

He'd hung up on her. Was this the same as slamming down the phone in the good old days? It wasn't quite as satisfying to press the end call button as it had been to slam down the receiver. She had hung onto the old-fashioned rotary phone in their house for as long as possible, she loved watching it spin around as she dialled the numbers.

She entered the Cafeteca café and ordered a giant latte, to drink on her way to work. Or should she sit down with it for ten minutes, on the terrace? She wasn't tired, but she needed a quick break. Andrada Vasiliu's parents would be picking up their daughter's body today. She walked out into the courtyard at the back of the café. There was just one free table, and she sat down with her back to the fence, so she could observe the other customers. It was mostly young people, excited about school restarting. She suspected that they would still be there in a few weeks, even after the start of school, skipping classes. Most of them were looking down at their phones, each wrapped up in their own world, barely speaking to each other, except for an occasional comment and giggle about something on-screen. Gigi looked at the birch leaves – they were just starting to turn yellow. The noise of traffic was very faint here in the courtyard.

She took the wallet out of her bag to pay at the bar and to order another coffee to go. When she returned to the courtyard, she saw a man bending over her table. She froze, incapable of either calling out or walking towards him to chase him away. He picked up a napkin which appeared to have been blown by the wind onto her table and threw it into the bin before leaving the café via the back gate. She was starting to panic a bit too easily. Her brain was clearly working overtime. She took her bag and left in a hurry.

She thought about Radu – he was probably anxious about Vlad reappearing. But she couldn't look after him too, he was old enough to handle things by himself. The days of the romantic couple – if those ever existed – were over now. She had work to do. She wanted to stay alert. She could feel that the predator was somewhere nearby. She couldn't see or hear him, but he was watching.

**

'Now you're busy with your new cases, we hardly ever get to see you.'

'Emil, how nice to see you! How was your holiday?'

'Great Nothing to do but sit in the sun and eat. The little one had sunstroke, so we got mad at each other, accused each other of neglect. Dana told me it was obviously my fault, since I took him into the water without his sunhat.'

'I thought you looked well-rested.'

'It was fine, actually. But I was a bit annoyed that you left me all on my own on my first day back.'

'I did send you a message that I might be running late.'

'And how is that supposed to help? I still had to work like a dog...'

'I'll get changed and finish off whatever else you have to do. Or I could write up the reports.'

'Except I've already written them up, since I had no idea when you'd be in. It's two o'clock, I'm going home in an hour.'

'I am so sorry,' she put a hand on his shoulder.

'I bet you are. Anyway, what's up? You have to catch me up on things. First, tell me about the conference.'

'God, what a drag that was, but Lemnaru insisted. I didn't stay long, just went and did my bit. Everyone seemed very bored. They probably just attend these things to spend three days in Braşov, who knows. Judging by the woman who spoke just before me, the attendees need to be paid to put up with that. But maybe it's just Radu annoying me...'

'Why?'

'He doesn't understand how busy I am.'

'Busy? You're planning to stay late today?'

'Yes, I'm seeing the parents of the first victim. They are coming to pick up the body. Or at least to sign the paperwork. I think the undertakers are picking up the body.'

'Ah, OK, I was hoping you could help me with something...'

'Ah, to punish me for not being here this morning?' Gigi laughed. 'What do you want me to do?'

'Remember the guy they brought in last month after he hanged himself? I'm writing an article about it and would like you to look over it.'

'Ah, yes, he was special because he didn't die of asphyxiation but of a stroke.'

'Exactly. Can you help?'

'Sure, email it to me and I'll send it back tomorrow.'

'It was a strange case... seeing the torn rope and him on the floor in a very peaceful position, his arms folded across his chest.'

'Do you think we're a bit strange, Emil, not like other people, to get excited about such things?'

'You are a freak, no doubt about that, but me, I'm just an ordinary man, going to work, listening to my tunes, trying to keep you up-to-date with things, in spite of your terrible taste in music... What's the matter? Why did you stop all of a sudden?'

'Something in my handbag just pricked my finger while I was searching for my phone. Look what I just found in here.' She showed Emil two badges.

One was a silvery metal magpie, about the size of one of her knuckles, with a white stripe running down the middle, while the other was small and round, with the number '13' in black on a white background.

'This is an old handbag, I don't think I've used it in years. I must have forgotten these inside, although I don't remember... Is this a magpie, do you think?'

'One for sorrow, two for joy,' Emil said and started humming, 'Three for a girl, four for a boy, five for silver, six for gold, seven for a secret never to be told.'

'What are you on about?'

'It's a children's rhyme, haven't you heard of it? It's been made into a song, here, let me find it on my playlist. Murder of One by Counting Crows.'

Emil put the song on and did some dance moves, then he stooped to look more closely at the badges, frowned and started tapping something on the keyboard.

'What are you doing?'

'Hang on a second, I want to see the full poem.' He found it and started reading it out loud without turning to look at her, his voice getting fainter and fainter as he went on.

'Eight for a wish, Nine for a kiss, Ten a surprise you should be careful not to miss, Eleven for health, Twelve for wealth, Thirteen beware it's the devil himself.'

They both fell silent for a while. 'That's a bit sinister,' said Gigi at last. He turned to her, blushing.

'I'm sorry, I should have kept my mouth shut.'

'Yes, well, too late now. I'll prepare for the parents.'

**

She tried to remember the names of Andrada's parents. Her mother was Elena, but she wasn't sure what her father was called. He was no longer limping, that she did notice.

'Hello again, I'm the pathologist, Gigi Alexa, I don't know if you remember.' They both nodded. 'Please come to my office to complete the paperwork.'

'I'll wait outside, if you don't mind, or go outside for a smoke.'

'Certainly, it's enough if Mrs Vasiliu signs.'

Gigi showed the mother into the office. She had discreetly turned the board with all the photos to face the wall. She had prepared some coffee.

'Would you like some coffee, Mrs Vasiliu?'

'No, thanks, I just want to get out of here as quickly as possible. And look after her. She's been shut up in here for so many days. I dreamed of her these last few nights. That she was a small child once more, calling for me, and I couldn't reach her.'

Gigi put her hand over Elena's hand. 'I understand.'

'I just wanted to tell you to check out Pompiliu Streza's alibi.'

'The director of the cultural centre?'

'He was in a relationship with my daughter. They'd been seeing each other for two years. He was married, but Andrada said he loved her.'

'We'll check that out, I promise.'

'Why haven't you done it already? What on earth are you doing? He's right under your noses.'

'Mrs Vasiliu, I can't give you any details about the case, but rest assured we are investigating all possible leads.'

Elena interrupted her, pushing the coffee away violently. The cup nearly flew off the table, but Gigi managed to stop it.

'Yes, all those phrases you use, "we're doing our best", "our utmost effort", as if that's any help. Do you have any children?'

'No.'

'Then you can't possibly understand how I feel! Just leave me alone!' Elena Vasiliu pulled the file towards her and rifled through the papers randomly. 'Tell me where the hell I'm supposed to sign!'

Gigi stood up but didn't accompany the woman out. Instead, she turned the board around, wrote Pompiliu Streza's name on a post-it and stuck it next to Andrada's picture. Then she phoned Matei to tell him about this meeting.

'I spoke to Streza myself and he didn't mention anything.'

'He might have thought we wouldn't find out.'

'I'll go see him again tomorrow. Meanwhile, get some rest.'

'See you tomorrow.'

She switched off her computer and all the lights, got changed and left the building. The air felt colder, slightly grubby. It was the second week of nasty, pestilent smells in town. Some people were protesting at the town hall, saying that they hadn't done a good job of covering and sanitising the accumulated rubbish at the dump on the edge of town. She was all too familiar with that smell of putrefaction. Although it didn't bother her back at the lab, she felt nauseous when she sensed it outside. She clenched her jaw, then tried to relax. Her mouth was filling up with saliva and she could feel her stomach rebelling. She spat out and held onto a fence as she bent over to throw up. A dog ran up to her, barking. She crept home with small, tight steps.

10

The Fifth

It was getting tight in the gallery. Party atmosphere. Flowers on the floor, people standing quietly at the entrance, holding bouquets, while from further inside you could hear syncopated jazz. The guests smoking outside were holding plastic flutes filled with champagne. The shop window contained the more spectacular installations, sculptures assembled from pieces of metal to resemble birds in flight. One of them had a body made out a spade, with wings fashioned from a series of knife blades, while the beak was the rusty spout of a watering can. Two others were entirely covered in blades to imitate feathers, with a body made out of a plain thick pipe. They were all supported by rods stuck into a base that could have been a piece from a circular saw. Inside the gallery there were several more such objects, some hanging on the walls, others suspended from the ceiling, so that visitors had to duck and mind their heads when walking among them.

The sculptor stood at the back of the room, facing his guests and explaining his work, alternating between simplicity (when he explained the materials) and grandeur (when discussing environmental concerns and disappearing species). His mission was to sound the alarm for the world, his metal sculptures were designed to make a lasting impression. His glasses had rusty metal frames and, when a journalist asked him about them, he waxed lyrical about the virtues of recycling.

People were walking in and out of the gallery space. There was a metal container on the improvised bar, where prosecco was being served. Two homeless men who had wandered inside in search of free food and drink were escorted from the premises by a security guard.

Nobody noticed him when he walked in and put an orchid in a pot down on the floor.

The name of this street had once been Custom House Road; during the Communist years, it was known as 7th November Road, and there were still some who called it that. Its official name was now Mureşenilor Street, and it was still very much work in progress, with many of the old buildings being renovated to their original splendour. For the time being, it resembled an elderly lady trying to bring some colour back into her life with lots of fancy make-up, but underneath you could detect the flaccid flesh and deep wrinkles. As soon as you walked a little into each passageway, the nasty smell from the sewers hit you, even in the chic restaurants that had been set up in nearly every other courtyard.

At night, petrolheads liked to show off and go racing down this road. They would rev their cars noisily as they came off the roundabout, draw breath as they entered the straight line and then race with engines screaming as soon as they reached the Catholic Church if they were coming from Livada Poştei or else the Black Church if they were coming from the opposite direction. They would repeat this feat until the locals called the police – which took at least half an hour.

The smaller car was a silver Audi TT, with custom-made purple lights. The other one was a Peugeot 308. It was after midnight. They were neck and neck when they heard the explosion. The window of the Europa Gallery was pulverised, with glass and metal shards raining on the cars just as they were passing. Their tyres scrunched on the sharp debris. No matter how proud they were of their driving skills, the two drivers could not avoid a collision. They managed to get out of the cars, surprised to find themselves relatively unharmed. Worried faces peered out of the windows nearby. The police arrived in no more than ten minutes.

11

When Gigi had got home the previous night, she'd found Radu sitting in the kitchen with a glass of wine and an almost empty bottle next to it. Hoping to avoid a confrontation, she asked him not to start an argument.

'Why is only your work important? Can you tell me that?'

'I'd rather not discuss this right now, Radu.'

'Well, when? When will you have time to discuss it?'

'Don't be like that! I'm busy, don't you get it?'

'What's so urgent about your job? Your "patients" aren't likely to go anywhere, are they? And they're not suffering.'

'It's far more than that, and you know it. I also have a responsibility towards their families.'

'Oh, of course, you're now the investigative supremo, without whom no crime in this city could ever be solved.'

'Please stop.'

'Am I wrong? Aren't they waiting for you to tell them what to do next?'

'You must be angry with me for not coming home earlier. But I really do have a lot to do and I'm not going to listen to you wallowing in self-pity because you are bored here by yourself. Go and find something to do, don't just wait for me.'

'Stop trying to tell me what I feel or what I should do. You think you're so clever. That guy come to tell you how he cannot live without you, is that it?'

'So it is about Vlad. You think I might go back to him?'

'You disgust me.'

'Radu, that's enough. You'll regret all this tomorrow.'

'Will I? Or else what? Eh?'

'Let's talk about this tomorrow.'

Her hands were trembling as she got undressed and got into bed. She heard him come into the bedroom later, but she had curled up tightly on her side of the bed and he didn't come near her. She was prepared to kick him out that very night if need be. The anger was stronger than the fear right then.

The next morning, she carefully poured the Greek coffee into her cup, trying not to disturb the thick grounds at the bottom of the pot. There wasn't much left, but she wasn't planning to make any for him.

Radu entered the kitchen, his gaze fixed on the floor.

'Good morning. Please forgive me. I don't think I remember everything I said last night, but it was all nonsense.'

'I would like you to leave, please.'

He reached for the coffee pot. 'I'm leaving very soon, I need to be at the surgery at eight.'

'No, I meant that I do not want you to come back here. I'll be working late today, and when I return, I expect you to have packed all your things and left. You can leave your set of keys in the postbox.'

'Wait, we have to talk.'

'I'm sorry, I can't. I've had enough of such nonsense. I've lived alone for most of my life, and I think I prefer it that way.'

'That's what you always say. I remember you saying it last night too. You always run away, or else you try to cancel or reject anyone who tries to get close to you. You are incapable of handling your feelings.'

'The only feeling I have right now for you is disdain. Please leave and let's not discuss this any further.'

'You'll regret it.'

'We'll just have to see, won't we? Please leave before I say anything more.'

'You think I'm scared of you? When I see your lip curling? I can see you despise me, so of course I'll go, but I think you're exaggerating. I knew this could never last when we last made up.'

'Might I remind you that we made up when your brother was being investigated by the police? So you had a good reason to want to be with me.'

'Why do you think I stayed then?'

'Who knows? I'm fun? Good-looking? Keep the house nice and tidy? I might not cook much, but you don't mind doing that yourself. And of course the sex was great. What more could you want?'

'I'll never understand which is your true face: the warm, gentle one or this one.'

'Does it matter?'

'Fine. I'll leave. But if I don't manage to pick up everything today, can I come over the next few days?'

'OK, but make sure you don't leave anything behind: your clothes, your stuff, your food, your wine.'

'What food?'

'The stuff you brought back from Amsterdam. If I find any of it, I'll throw it out. And I know how much you hate wasting food. The two remaining wine bottles are in the kitchen cupboard, by the way.'

'Are you crazy? What wine are you talking about?'

'The Cabernet bottles. With the horse's head.'

'I didn't buy those. I found them in front of your door when I arrived that evening. I thought you had ordered them specially.'

She knew she hadn't ordered anything, but she couldn't bear a lengthy discussion now.

'Anyway, what I meant was take everything that's yours. And let me know when you plan to drop by, so that I can make sure I won't be there.'

Radu put the coffee pot back on the table. He took his coat from the hanger then came forward to shake Gigi's hand.

'Thank you for the time we spent together.'

His face had the fixed smile of an estate agent, but she could see his shoulders sagging. She stuck out her hand and shook his. Then, when the door had closed behind him, she wiped her fingers on her pyjama bottoms. She poured the remainder of the cold coffee on top of the coffee in her cup and lit a cigarette.

This was not how she'd imagined celebrating her birthday. While Radu was in the Netherlands, she had even tentatively planned to organise something. Maybe that's why he had wanted to ask her out last night. She'd have liked to go for a spa and massage session for couples at Hotel Alpin, but had waited to see if he was preparing some kind of surprise. And then she started wondering if he even remembered that it was her birthday. But he had annoyed the hell out of her last night, wallowing in drunken self-pity and jealousy. She deserved a better present than that.

By the time the phone rang a quarter of an hour later, she had already smoked three cigarettes.

'Happy birthday, Gigi.'

'Matei, how nice to hear from you so early in the morning. Tell me quickly what you want, because I need to go to the toilet.'

'We're on the phone, you can go and talk at the same time.'

'Nooo. Too embarrassing.'

'OK, anyway, the idea is that things have taken a turn for the worse. There's been an explosion on Mureşenilor.'

'Really? I thought you were just calling to wish me happy birthday. Was quite impressed that you'd remembered.'

'Yes, of course, but I haven't got any present for you.'

'Never mind that. So tell me, what explosion?'

'An art gallery. Around two in the morning.'

'Any victims?'

'No, although two idiots managed to crash into each other as they were racing down the road.'

'How on earth?'

'Their tyres got slashed when they drove over the metal and glass debris on the road, and they lost control. They found the remains of a home-made bomb inside the gallery.'

'So why are we involved?'

'Marcel and three other investigators have been moved to this case. It's top priority, potential terrorist act. So it's a task force something or other.'

'Really?' Gigi sighed.

'Yep. Major headache. I spoke to Tomescu, who of course has been brought in to coordinate everything. And he said you should take some time off from your day job and work with us full-time on this.'

'Starting when?'

'Today.'

'Can he send a request or document to my boss, so that I have a good reason to do so?'

'Sure, I'll let him know. We'll email it to Lemnaru and copy you in. I hope he's not going to expect a signed paper document in triplicate? OK, so I'll see you at the police station asap.'

'As soon as I can. But could you send a car or come and get me yourself? I've created a board myself with pictures and connections and I'd like to bring it in.'

'Is it heavy?'

'No, I just stuck everything on a polystyrene board, roughly the size of a flipchart sheet.'

'Fine. Let me know when you're ready and I'll arrange something.'

She went to see Lemnaru after the email request arrived. It was easier not to ask for permission, to simply wait until he received the email and called her into his office to shout at her. Gigi stood before him, careful to not allow any negative expression on her face. She knew that the whole building could hear him call her an opportunist, and tell her that she only dreamt of a career path that had nothing to do with her actual current work, that he would kick her out and then she'd find out if the police would give her a full-time position. She didn't budge, even when she could feel droplets of his saliva on her face. She wanted to wipe herself clean, or shout back, but it was best to remain silent. The system could pull you down all too easily, and Lemnaru had all the power. She silently handed him her request form for unpaid leave, but he yelled even louder and said she should take her remaining annual leave.

In the end, it all worked out exactly as she had hoped, but she kept her head down and tried not to smile, as if the victory was all his. As she walked out of the room, she mentioned that it was her birthday, just to see on his face the slight regret that he had overreacted.

She picked up her board and documents and went down to the car.

'Thank you for coming yourself to pick me up.'

'There was no one else I could send, if I'm honest,' Matei smiled.

'Is it that bad?'

'Oh yes. It's anti-terrorist task force all the way, they've even given it a code name: *Iron Bird,* can you believe it?'

'So how many are left working with us?'

'Six, including us. But we're the only full-timers and one of the remaining four is Nicu, who is a real newbie, more of a driver really than an investigator.'

'And the other three?'

'Andrei, Mihai and Robert.'

'I think I know them. Robert especially, seems helpful and intelligent. We don't even have Paul for IT?'

'Tomescu said he would be allowed to help us if we have anything concrete.'

'Fair enough. Shall we go see Streza now? Or have you been to see him already?'

'Not yet.'

They parked outside the police station. It was still warm; autumn could be so beautiful in this city. Gigi got out of the car and looked up towards Mount Tîmpa.

'The woods are gorgeous at this time of year.'

'I keep meaning to go for a run along the path below Tîmpa, but I end up just doing a tour around the block of flats in Tractoru. Maybe I should take my running shoes with me and go for a jog after I finish work.'

'At ten at night?'

'Oh, you do know how to crush people's dreams!'

'That's my specialty.'

**

The Reduta Cultural Centre occupied the building which had housed the city's first theatre back in the eighteenth century. Gigi struggled to open the heavy door. She could hear Matei chuckling behind her.

'Female emancipation can be tough at times. Couldn't you wait for me?'

'Oh, shush.'

Their voices echoed in the empty marble hallway. As they went upstairs, she shuddered seeing the green-black granite on the walls.

'Don't you think it looks a bit like the morgue? Or a funeral parlour?'

Matei raised an eyebrow. Pompiliu Streza appeared at the top of the stairs.

'Hello, I was expecting you. Let's find a place to talk.'

They followed Streza into a small room right next to the stairs they had just climbed. A dressing table stood opposite the door, and a run-down armchair. Gigi flopped down on it, while Matei pulled up a chair. Streza had to content himself with the stool in front of the dressing table, and only turned to look at them once he started talking:

'I prefer being here without any onlookers, thank you for your understanding, Inspector.'

'Dr Regina Alexa is working with us on this investigation, I hope you don't mind if she sits in on this conversation.'

'Of course. No problem.'

'This is just a conversation,' Gigi clarified once more. 'We want to hear your side of the story, because we're dealing with a delicate situation.'

'I'm willing to cooperate and tell you everything I know. I'm finding all this quite difficult.'

Pompiliu Streza looked as woebegone as a beaten dog. The man was around 45-50 years old. His hair was slightly longer in front, so that he could sweep it back over the bald patch at the top of his head. He arranged his hair before continuing: 'I think I can guess what brought you here. You said you wanted to discuss the special relationship I had with Andrada?'

The others nodded, so he continued.

'We rarely met up, at most once a week. I would go to her place after the show here, after ten at night. I didn't go that evening. Andrada was getting tired of our relationship. She told me when she came to the theatre that day, two hours before the show. Not exactly breaking up with me, but she was fed up. I never promised her anything. We never saw each other outside work, we didn't communicate.' Long pause. 'This was her dressing room. There's no trace of her left anywhere. At the most, a couple of posters.'

'Thank you, Mr Streza. Do you know if she was in a relationship with anyone else?'

'Not really. I told you, we didn't talk much.'

Matei got up and walked towards the window, then turned suddenly to look at Streza: 'Can you tell me what you did after Andrada left that evening on the first of September?'

'We all left together. There were two other people other than Andrada and myself: the technical director, who did the lighting, and the box office manager. The three of us went to my car, which was parked on Bălcescu Boulevard, and she walked off by herself. We said goodbye at the bar itself, and we walked down the alley between Gott and Gaura Dulce.'

'I'm afraid I'm going to have to ask what time you arrived home.'

'Well, I didn't look at my watch, Inspector, but I think it was after midnight.'

'Anyone who can confirm that?'

'My wife,' whispered Streza. 'Do you need to talk to her?'

'Yes. She can give a statement at the police station.'

'But could you please not tell her about Andrada? I beg you.' Streza had picked up a piece of paper from the dressing table and was ripping it to shreds.

Gigi got up too and headed for the door. 'In principle, we don't have to present the whole context to her...'

'Thank you.'

'Please come to the station to give a formal statement yourself, Mr Streza.'

He remained seated, his eyes fixed on the ground, as they left the room.

'Don't you think he should be taking it more to heart?' asked Matei.

'What do you mean?'

'This is a woman with whom he was close. He held her in his arms, maybe had feelings for her. His reaction was rather neutral, as if she had been a mere acquaintance or work colleague.'

'I think he's afraid, Matei.'

'Afraid of what?'

'Of his wife. He cares more about what will happen to him than what happened to Andrada.'

'Cold-blooded...'

'Preservation instinct, I think. Typical.'

'So we've wasted our time?'

'You didn't think we'd solve the case today, did you?' Gigi laughed.

**

The room where they had moved all the noticeboards measured more than 20 square metres, with windows opening up to the inner courtyard and also to the hillside of Dealul Melcilor.

'You could go jogging here instead of Tîmpa, couldn't you?'

'I did consider it. But imagine coming back all sweaty... everyone staring at me...'

'Doesn't quite fit your image as chief of police, right?'

'Not really, no.'

Matei was always so concerned about what other people thought. For him, it was all about behaving the way others expected him to behave, that was the only way to win someone's respect. For the first time in his life, he was vaguely tempted to let his hair grow a bit, instead of shaving it all off. He'd fallen into that habit in high school, simply shaving his head while he was in the shower. He had changed his outfit today, although he hadn't gone as far as putting on a suit. At least he now wore a shirt underneath his jacket. He took his jacket off before moving the tables and chairs around the room. Gigi was sitting near the window, watching him, how his biceps seemed to tense up in the short-sleeved shirt far more than the act of moving the furniture warranted.

'I assume you don't really need me to help.'

'Nearly done, don't worry.'

The three boards they had were nearly full.

'Where would you like me to set up yours?'

'Here, let me show you. There's a lot of duplication, so I'll take down the things that you already have and supplement them with some of the stuff from my autopsies. I'll leave this up here...'

The freestanding noticeboard was somewhat rickety and starting to sway when Gigi grabbed it.

'Are you OK?' Matei caught her.

'I thought I would feel more inspired if I turned around and closed my eyes. Then I lost my balance.'

'Are you feeling dizzy?'

'I suddenly got this incontestable sensation that it's the same perpetrator.'

'But you have no evidence for that.'

'No.'

The door opened suddenly, noisily, and Tomescu burst into the room.

'Hello! Settled in?'

'Er, yes. Are you trying to make small talk?' asked Gigi with a smile.

'I'm sorry we had to move you out of the main room, but the explosion now takes absolute priority. Happy birthday, Gigi. I wanted to bring you flowers, you know.'

Gigi raised an eyebrow. 'Thank you. Matei told me about the bomb.'

'Can you tell us anything more about it, Vlad?' Matei invited him to sit down.

'Not much. You probably know most of it already. It's a simple home-made bomb, anyone could have done it, classical recipe. The materials can be obtained at any hardware or DIY store. You can find instructions on the internet. It will be a major job to check all the sales in these stores and it probably won't add up too much. We can check the dates and times when these materials were bought, maybe check CCTV, but if they were bought a while ago, we won't find much. They keep CCTV recordings for a month at most.'

'What about the gallery?'

'Someone is going through all the pictures, there were two official photographers there, invited by the artist, plus all the guests taking pictures. Everyone has a camera on their mobile phone nowadays. We'll organise a press conference and ask all those attending the opening of the exhibition to send us their pictures. We're going to need so many bodies working on this. And we don't really know what we're looking for.'

'Where was the bomb hidden?'

'Thank you, Gigi, for coming straight to the point as usual. Your style can be annoying at times, as if we hadn't thought of things. Don't frown, I'm used to it by now. Yes, so there were lots of flower arrangements and pots on a low table and on the floor, and that's where the explosion took place.'

'Any damage to the neighbouring buildings?' Gigi continued, pretending not to notice Vlad's wink.

'They're more or less OK. There is a rental flat above the gallery, luckily no one was in it. The windows towards the street got smashed. The buildings to either side are fine. It was a crazy night for the emergency services though, I think everyone in that part of town must have called them. I'll be holding a press conference about the bomb right now. If they ask me anything about your cases, I will just say that we're working on them and haven't got any updates for the time being.'

'Are you going, or just letting Alina speak on your behalf? I think she might struggle to control the masses.' Matei seemed to be suggesting what Vlad should do.

'I'll go. It's a complex matter.'

'Hang on! Did the explosion have anything to do with the sculptor? Who is he?'

'Andreas Demeter. Half German, half Hungarian. He was interviewed by Marcel, I spoke to him a bit as well. He says he hasn't got any enemies, but this exhibition did provoke some envy. He toured with it all summer: Berlin, Vienna, Budapest, and has now finally reached Braşov. Apparently, the local press had been bigging it up for months, that he was back in his hometown after being fêted throughout Europe. That's why it was so busy out there last night. The guy is really upset that he lost all his work. It was blown to smithereens, we couldn't recover much of it. He never received any threats or anonymous messages or anything. Only congratulations. But we will dig deep and find the culprit, don't you worry.'

He left. Gigi finally broke the silence: 'Nice of him to tell us all that.'

'Nice my arse! I'm the head of police here and I've been shunted off onto the sidetrack. Call that nice?' Matei slammed his file down onto the table.

'You are right. I'm sorry.'

'I've had enough. I'm going and sitting in on that press conference myself!'

**

Alina let her hair fall down her back, then grabbed it firmly and twisted it into a bun. Her black hair shone in the neon lights. She looked at herself in the mirror, squinting a bit, then took out the lipstick she had managed to rescue just before it fell down the drain in the basin. She put on the pale pink lipstick and smiled. There would no doubt be pictures taken at the press conference. She took a step back, checked her profile, then brushed down the lapels of her suit.

'Sub-officer Alina Moise will give you a quick summary of the case,' she heard her own voice echo around the bathroom fitted with white tiles from floor to ceiling. She had been delighted by her promotion, although she suspected it would be her last one. If she wanted to progress, she would have to move to a different department rather than the press office, but she was not in the mood for that, although she knew that her job wasn't considered a prestigious one. The other police officers thought that she and her young and rather clumsy colleague were wasting their time, that they didn't have much to do. Little did they know that any text, even a mere couple of sentences, had to be approved by them before being sent out to the press. It had to meet the approval of the chief of police too. It was easier working with Matei than Vlad, who always had some criticism or comment to make: that the message was unclear, or that it was too direct, so all his press releases ended up sounding the same, vague and pompous.

Tomescu was now back and already taking over. So far he had not said anything about her relationship with Matei, but maybe he had been told something. There was a risk that she might have to be transferred elsewhere. Anyway, she wouldn't worry about that now. If Matei didn't mention it, it meant that he could handle it somehow. She would have liked to move in with him, maybe even in his flat that he cared so much about. Except that it was a one-bedroom flat and she wanted kids. Soon, because she was thirty-nine and had no time to waste. She could sell her flat in Râşnov, that she had bought with a mortgage ten years ago. It might not be worth much, but it would help them buy a two-bedroom flat at least.

She started looking through her papers once more. The door opened slowly.

'I'm sorry, I thought there was nobody here.'

'It's fine, Bianca, you can come in. The toilets are free.'

She and Matei had tried to hide their relationship, but most people knew about it. She was sure her colleagues regarded her with caution rather than respect.

The room on the second floor where the press conference was taking place was not quite large enough. All the newspapers and local radio stations had sent their correspondents. Alina knew most of them. The guy from Brașov News had called her for a scoop early that morning. He had posted something about the explosion on their site even before she had prepared a formal statement. She refused to talk to him, but she was sure he had someone on the inside leaking information. She hadn't yet been able to find out who it was – possibly Bianca.

Tomescu was already sat at the table, going through some papers. Matei was staring at the people coming into the room, nodding slightly whenever he spotted someone he knew, occasionally even attempting a faint smile. She sat down next to him.

'I'm glad you're here. I thought it was going to be just me and him.'

'I told him that I was not OK with being sidelined.'

'And?'

'Well, I'm here aren't I?'

Vlad Tomescu leaned over Matei to address Alina directly.

'You can start, and then please let me answer any questions. You call them out, as we decided.'

Alina stood up, tapped her papers on the table and, with a very earnest face, began:

'Good afternoon. Thank you all for coming in such high numbers. I am sub-officer Alina Moise, and here with me we have Chief Inspector Matei Vălean, chief of police, and Superintendent Vlad Tomescu, on loan from the Police HQ in Bucharest. During the early hours of the 10th of September, at 02:20 to be precise, there was an explosion at the Europa Gallery, the exhibition centre for the artists belonging to the Artists' Union. The explosion pulverised the window and hurled metal exhibits across distances of up to ten metres. Two cars were passing on Mureșenilor Street at that time, and they crashed into each other after driving over the metal debris on the road. There were no fatalities. This case is our absolute priority at the moment, and the police are working hard to find those responsible for the incident. If you have any questions, Superintendent Vlad Tomescu is here to answer them.'

Alina pointed at the reporter from Braşov News, who had raised his hand before she even finished speaking.

'Petrache from Braşov News. Do we know if this was a terrorist act or not?'

'We consider all situations involving explosives deployed with the purpose of causing damage to be terrorist acts,' Vlad said without bothering to stand up.

Petrache tried to squeeze in another question without asking Alina for permission, but she intervened. 'Mr Petrache, please wait for your opportunity to ask any additional questions. Now Mrs Andone from Braşov TV please.'

Aurora Andone was small and blonde, with a child-like round face, but appearances were deceptive in her case. 'We have two additional cases of violent murders. If you are focusing all your efforts on this terrorist act which didn't even claim any victims, what will happen with the other cases? As far as I know, you still have zero suspects.'

Tomescu put his hand on Matei's arm, to indicate that he would answer the question.

'We have a team dedicated to those two cases, led by Chief Inspector Vălean. His team has all the resources they need. According to Law 535 from 2004 and the amendments from 2019, we are looking at what has been defined as a terrorist act. We have to treat this with the utmost caution. Since public safety is at stake here, we will make sure that the police collaborate with other public services to ensure that we get to the bottom of this.'

'Since you mention the law, Superintendent... I am Vasile Baicu from ProTV, and apologies, Alina, for jumping in. Can you tell us if there is any particular reason why it was Andreas Demeter's sculpture exhibition that was targeted by the bomber? Do you think it is a hate crime against the sculptor because he is of Hungarian origin?'

'We are all on high alert, which means that we are also very careful about making assumptions. Therefore, I would like to recommend caution in what you say as well. If you do read the law I mentioned, you will see that distributing false news and rumours that destabilise the situation could be punishable by law.'

'Will you conduct the investigation yourself or will it be led by the security services?' Petrache called out his question without raising a hand.

'This information is of no interest to the public. All our institutions will work together to find a solution to this unusual situation. Next question, please.'

There were some titters of laughter in the room. The former Justice Minister Florin Iordache had used that phrase so frequently two years before, when faced with huge numbers of protesters out on the streets, that his nickname had become Next Question Please. Tomescu smiled to disguise his embarrassment.

'Yes, I'm glad I made you laugh. But it is a challenging situation, I'll admit that. We will keep you informed, but so far there is nothing much to report. I think we had better end things here. Thank you.'

The murmurs in the room grew louder, but Tomescu signalled to the two other police officers to follow him as he left the room.

**

When Matei got back to the case room, Gigi was still standing at the window.

'How was it?' she said, coming forward to sit down facing him.

'What did you expect? Tomescu wanted to act tough, but he made a mistake and everyone laughed at him.'

'What mistake?'

'He sounded terribly like Next Question Please. Someone asked him something he didn't like, he lost his nerve, and it slipped out.'

Gigi burst out laughing, 'Like hell!'

'You can imagine the headlines tomorrow.'

'Did they ask about our crimes?'

'Of course. A female reporter – I've seen her in action before and she's a real bulldog. She said that no one died in the explosion, so why don't we focus our efforts on the murders? While Tomescu went on and on about terrorist attacks being our number one priority, as if we were back in the days of the revolution and sniper attacks. Pure nonsense!'

'Why? You think that it was a personal vendetta against Demeter?'

'Not sure, but that might be the case.'

'OK, but in the meantime, what shall we do about our cases? We have nothing to go on, Matei.'

'I know. We need to keep on digging... and waiting.'

'Now that *does* sound sinister...'

12

The Sixth

The three towers gleamed so brightly in the sunshine, it looked like someone had just passed by and given them a fresh coat of paint. The crowds were jostling in the registration area, with the tables displaying the letters of the alphabet where the runners could pick up their kit. People were smiling at each other, often in recognition. They would soon take their place to start the Knossos half-marathon, with the finishing line in Heraklion. For those who would make it to the end.

In the heat, they estimated that the event would take around three hours, even for the slowest runners. The temperature was already 22 degrees centigrade, and it wasn't even nine o'clock yet. By midday it would be over 30 degrees, but that didn't worry him. He wasn't afraid of anything in the world. He felt a joy deep down, could feel things settling down inside. He was in complete control and his body was gathering strength. He felt brave.

He thanked the young woman at the registration desk several times, she wished him the best of luck and said she would love to see him after the race. Her curly black hair was held back by a yellow hairband. He could imagine her on all fours, the hair hanging over her face and the hairband stuck in her mouth like the bit of a bridle. But he had something else to do first, no matter how tempting that image was. He had noticed lately that he was having more and more inappropriate, even disturbing thoughts, which might distract him from what he had to do. He asked the girl for her number, mostly to make her feel better. She wrote it down on a piece of paper which she tore from the block in front of her, after searching frantically for something appropriate to write on. She told him her name was Elena.

'Of course it's Elena, you're the most beautiful one,' he said, taking the paper and giving it a kiss, with a broad smile on his face.

She would probably wait for him at the finishing line, dream of spending a few days with this foreign athlete, a holiday romance. As soon as he was out of eyesight, he threw the paper in the bin and went to the starting line, where the other runners were warming up, doing knee bends, stretching, lifting their arms up. There was a scent of excitement, freshness, deodorant, soon to be replaced by the smell of effort, heavy sweat and the sticky plastic smell of their elite running clothes.

He set off at a pace that he knew he could sustain right until the end. The first part of the race was quite busy, but those who had taken their training seriously would soon break off from the rest of the pack. He kept his eyes firmly a few metres ahead of him, not really looking at what was happening around him. The pack right at the front was sparse, consisting of thirty runners at the most, so he stuck to the middle group of runners, far more numerous. Every man for himself now. He would have liked to be with the ones in front, and felt slightly sorry he had not trained hard enough to be among them. He didn't like being too ambitious when he had other things to do, and although he was a regular runner, this was his first half-marathon.

The water stations with water bottles and energy drinks were situated every fifty metres or so. As soon as he approached a stand, a volunteer would reach out to him, a bottle in one hand and a cup in the other. He took them both and ran on. He swigged a few gulps of water from the bottle and poured the one from the cup onto his head, but that was a mistake, because he was sweating and his skin soon started itching. Nevertheless, he managed to maintain his pace and stick to the middle pack, which was spreading out a little as they reached the seafront in Heraklion. Although the temperature was still boiling hot, the proximity to the sea had cooled the air, you could breathe a little better, even feel a light breeze.

By now there were gaps of a couple of metres or so between runners. Ahead of him he saw a well-built man, wearing blue shorts and a white top. His long blond hair was tied back in a ponytail. He overtook him, sprinting a little, then squatted down pretending to tighten his shoelaces, so he could steal a better look at him. The other man ignored him completely, too preoccupied with counting out his breaths and steps. He could feel his heart filling with joy, as he inhaled more deeply.

He accelerated once more, overtook the man again, then took two cups of water at the next station. He stopped a short way ahead, bent down as if he had something in his shoes, took the phial he had hanging around his neck and poured the liquid from it into one of the cups. He balanced the two cups and started moving slowly. Meanwhile, the man he had been observing was approaching, the frown on his forehead getting more pronounced. When the man drew level with him, he offered him one of his cups. The blond man stepped sideways to avoid him in the first instance, but he ran lightly alongside him with his hand stretched out until he took it. He signalled that they should clink cups, and the man nodded and even smiled. He heard a 'thank you' and they both downed their cups in one, then ran on. He would have liked to see him fall. He would have liked to be certain. But he kept on running for a few more metres, then he left the race route and headed back into town. He went directly to his hotel. The luggage was packed, he had a change of clothes to hand after a long shower. His mission was over. He had no doubt it had been successful, but he would have liked to know more. It was the kind of thing that got some coverage.

He was as tanned as the other tourists in the airport terminal. His light blue chinos were so similar to those of other travellers that it almost looked like a uniform. He wouldn't stand out in any way. He joined the line at security with a clear conscience, reassuring them that he had no liquids. Then he stopped at the Duty Free and, after wandering down some aisles, chose a banal fragrance, Allure by Chanel, for which he paid cash.

He checked the news after boarding the plane, but nothing had appeared yet. He switched off his phone and snuggled deeper in his chair, hoping to snooze all the way to his destination.

13

Gigi woke up with a headache, unable to even open her eyes. Her first attempt to do so resulted in what felt like pinpricks to her eyelids. She gingerly touched her right temple, which appeared to be the source of the pain. She felt blindly for her phone on the bedside table, but was only able to look at it with her left eye. 5:45 and it wasn't yet light outside. The sunrise was a mere good intention on the horizon. Morty was snoring on the bed beside her. She made an effort to open her right eye, bent over the cat and blew in his face. The cat flinched but did not get out of bed when she did.

The wooden floor was cold as she walked barefoot down the hallway. She should have put underfloor heating in. She found her slippers in the kitchen. She drew the curtain, not a soul to be seen on the street yet, but soon it would be buzzing, since it was the first day of school. There would be cars parked on her street for sure: all those parents who had to accompany their offspring to school at least on this day.

Her own parents must have taken her to school on the first day, but she could not remember them ever being by her side. And yet she hadn't really felt abandoned. Maybe if it had felt like an important day she would have remembered. Who knows what the rules are for storing our memories? Why do we cling onto some memories and not others, and at what point do we decide which falls into which category? Why do we press delete on some memories? Perhaps we don't do that deliberately, it just happens and then we scramble around to justify things.

She pressed the button on the coffee machine and waited for the aroma to envelop her. It had been Radu who made the coffee usually. The first few days he brought it to her in bed, which exasperated her. She had always been careful not to hurt him when she refused the coffee, just like he'd tried to swallow her culinary experiments without any comment. Of course he would have preferred her to be aware of his unspoken wishes, all couples seem to expect the other person to be a mind-reader. She didn't miss him at all. It would be a while yet before she started missing the warmth of having someone to curl up with in bed. Maybe during the winter. Except maybe by then she would have invested in an electric blanket.

This had been her first weekend off since the investigations had started. Two days with nothing to do. She was almost tempted to check if they needed her to do some overtime shifts at the mortuary. She could have worked on the proposal for her doctoral thesis, but she really wanted to go out, breathe in some fresh air, get some new ideas. On Saturday she had gone for a walk in Şchei, with just a small backpack and a half-litre bottle of water, which she had nearly emptied by the time she got to Solomon's Rocks. There were far too many people hiking there, so she wasn't in the mood to continue up the mountain to Poiana.

She had passed by the house where Andrada Vasiliu died. The windows were closed, shutters drawn, the house had aged suddenly. She went around the back of the houses on Vrancei Street, but quickly turned back. She didn't like the cold and damp of the forest. She had vaguely hoped to find some new clue, something that might lead to a revelation. She was still not sure what the killer had used to pull the fingernail out. It must have been something more precise than an ordinary pair of pliers. Possibly a bit curved too.

Something like an eyelash curler, that would have been the right shape.

When she got to the police headquarters, she passed by Matei's office.

'Good morning, Matei.'

'Morning to you too,' he replied without lifting his head from his laptop.

'Any news?'

'Don't know. This quiet worries me. We've made no progress whatsoever. Did you bring some coffee?'

'Here, have some,' she handed him a paper cup.

'Thanks. How are you, had a good weekend?'

''So-so. I slept late and then tried to clear my head, get some new ideas. I was planning to walk all the way up to Poiana, but didn't get very far. What about you?'

'You remember that this guy showed up at one of our briefings complaining that someone had pushed him on Postăvaru?'

'Vaguely. Why?'

'He's been making waves everywhere. Complaining that nobody pursued the matter after he made the statement at the hospital. He came to see us as soon as he was out of hospital to leave a formal complaint. He fell from quite a height and was extremely lucky to survive. Anyway, do you remember our friend the lawyer Albulescu? I don't know how the hell he of all people, got involved in this, but they're suing us for dereliction of duty.'

'Hang on, how come?'

'I'll be fucked if I have any idea how they can justify it, pardon my language.'

'Don't worry. Is it you personally that he's complaining about?'

'The chief of police. There's an article here: "The police in Braşov are incapable of solving serious cases, and yet they ignore all the other so-called minor cases". That's the subtitle, the actual headline is "Matei Vălean falls into a pit of incompetence".'

'Catchy! What can be done?'

'The article appeared today, but on Saturday I spoke to Cezar Condurache, the guy who fell. He really had incredible luck, tumbled among rocks and trees and only broke his arm. He says he was pushed but he didn't see anyone.'

'So what can we do?'

'I've got two people checking the CCTV from the cable car for that day, if what he says is true. But of course the attacker could have climbed up and gone down on foot.'

'That's all we needed.'

'Exactly.'

'They've reduced our numbers further, is it just the two of us on these cases?'

'Two and a half, with a share of Andrei Filip.'

'Is Tomescu progressing on his investigation?'

'Nope. The mayor apparently called to spur him on, while the bosses from Bucharest are demanding daily progress reports. I think he's scared to death. He's got another week and if he doesn't come up with the goods, they'll replace him. He asked me to tell you he's waiting for you in his office.'

'You're kidding?'

'No, I swear. Go and see what he wants.'

'You're smiling, you must be joking...'

'No, I'm simply amused that you're white as a sheet.'

'Fine, I'll go see him. Is he still in the office on the third floor? I was expecting him to move somewhere more fancy.'

'Still there. Maybe he doesn't want to shake things up too much while he's only on secondment.'

She walked up the stairs slowly, pausing after every step, holding onto the handrail. She had been tempted to wear black again that morning, but in the end had decided on her blue skirt with big pink flowers, a yellow T-shirt and a magenta-coloured cardigan. As usual, she was wearing trainers. She took a deep breath before walking into his office.

'Good morning. Vlad, Matei told me you wanted to see me.'

'Hi, I just wanted to say that I am counting on you for those two cases.'

'On me?'

'Yes, I think we need a bit of lateral thinking there. You are the one who keeps saying that each criminal is also a victim, and that seems to fit those cases. Have you had any more ideas during the weekend?'

'Not really. I walked past the house again. I had a moment of anxiety there, not sure why. Maybe because of you.'

'Really? It's been more than a year...'

'Just joking, I think. Are you sure you didn't send me those flowers?'

'You still haven't found out who they're from?'

'No, although admittedly I haven't gone to great lengths to discover that. I could go with a warrant demanding to be shown all their tapes.'

'That would be an abuse of authority, you know.'

'I know, that's why I'm not doing it.'

'Would you like to go out for dinner tonight?'

Gigi frowned, then laughed, 'Is that why you called me here?'

'No. I swear. But when I saw you... we could talk about things in more detail.'

'I was sort of expecting something like this, I was even half-thinking of accepting. But I can't. Not today.'

'I just want us to be friends. Like we were once.'

'Not sure if I can.'

'So you still feel something for me?'

'Yes, a certain unease when I am around you. I thought I was over it, but...'

'Fine, let's change the subject then. But think about it, let me know if you reconsider. It can be a professional dinner, not too formal, not too personal. I really miss picking your brains.'

'Let's get back to our cases, shall we? What would you like us to do next? I've run out of ideas. That's what is most frustrating. We've worked ourselves to the bone, checking all the contacts, going into their online accounts, speaking to all their acquaintances, nothing. The killer is not part of their social circle. I still think it's the same person. Yet these women never had anything in common. I can't find a single connection.'

'What does this mean?'

'That we have to wait for something else to happen.'

'Has Matei told you about the papers?'

'He did. And you're notorious too now, they've made a meme of you on social media saying "Next Question Please"...'

Tomescu lowered his head. 'I've seen that. I feel really bad about it.'

'Don't worry. It won't last. People forget easily.'

'Is there anything I can do to help you guys on your cases? If I get a breather, because I have to write daily reports for the Minister and the Police HQ in Bucharest, as if the bomb investigation weren't enough to keep me busy.'

'Any developments there?'

'None, other than that we know how the bomb was made and that anyone could have got hold of the components quite easily.'

'I'm sorry. I'll do my best on my side of things then.'

14

The Seventh

He would have liked to take the window seat, but a young woman had a paper boarding card in her hand and kept looking at it and at him, then turned to check all the other rows of seats before finally turning and asking him if he was sitting in her seat by any chance. She had rather thin, very straight hair covering most of her face, which she kept pushing back behind her ears. He tried to convince her to swap, but she proved surprisingly tenacious, so he had to give way.

He was too pumped up from his success at the race to want to start a fight. Fate had been kind to him on this trip. It meant he was on the right path and his mission would succeed.

He thought nobody clapped after a landing anymore, but he woke up just as they did so. Then they all stood up at once, taking their bags down from the overhead lockers. He was in no rush, he knew that the two buses wouldn't leave until all the passengers had disembarked, so what was the point in pushing forward? The girl with the mousy hair was far ahead of him, she hadn't even bothered to say goodbye.

**

He pressed the buttons on the remote locking system and by the time he got to his car, the windows were down.

He flung himself into the driver's seat and felt like singing out loud. Rested and tanned as he was after his Greek success. Although yesterday he had wasted all day in Bucharest, wandering around Cişmigiu Park early in the morning, but then retreating indoors when it got hot. He had been expecting the streets to be less busy at two in the morning, but that wasn't the case. It was his second evening in a row out hunting. He was running out of time, he had to strike it rich tonight.

He saw a man in the distance, swaying from one side of the pavement to another. He slowed down and stopped next to him.

'Hello there.'

The man tried to turn round, but had to take a step back to prop himself up against a wall.

'Evenin'.'

'How can I get to the Arch of Triumph?'

'Wha'?'

'Arch of Triumph!' he shouted.

'Turn and then right. I think. My, I'm dizzy...' He leant against a lamppost.

'I'm not from Bucharest, would you mind getting into the car and showing me the way? And then I can take you home if you like.'

He opened the passenger door, then decided he needed to get out of the car. 'Here, let me help you in.'

He didn't mind the smell. He drew a deep breath. There was some vomit on the man's clothes, but no piss. The car wouldn't suffer too much. He held the man under his armpits and sat him down in the passenger seat, then lifted up his feet.

'You're tickling me, man.'

'Sorry. Do you know where you live?'

'Course I do, I live there! On Lizeanu Street. That's where.'

'Fine, we'll go there. What have you been celebrating tonight?'

He let his passenger do the talking, merely agreeing with him every now and then. Of course it was normal for him to go out for drinks with his friends on pay day, naturally his wife was a bitch and he should pay no attention to what she said, a man has to relax with his mates, not follow her around all the time. Besides, it was his hard-earned money, he had the right to do with it as he pleased. He found himself almost imitating the man's accent and vocabulary. The drunkard had nearly fallen asleep when he held out a bottle.

'What this? Water? Want me to rust away?'

'Juice. Vitamins. Take a good long sip.'

The drunk man emptied the bottle, then burped loudly. 'To our health!'

He bent over almost instantly, then lurched back and closed his eyes. His breathing became increasingly ragged, and after a few minutes it slowed down. By the time the car stopped, he was barely breathing.

The driver parked the car with two wheels on the pavement, got out and lifted the legs out first, then pulled his arms hard. With one heave, he grabbed the man by his middle and lifted him up. It was only two steps to the gate of the building site, which he attempted to kick open. It stuck. The drunkard murmured something, he was unstable, slipping from his grasp, so he had to put him down to undo the rudimentary wire fastening. He stepped carefully over the plank laid down at the entrance and switched his torch on. Just as he thought, the hole in the ground was enormous, like the rapacious mouth of a beast of prey. He turned and picked up his load again, then slid him a little over the edge of the hole. Before leaving, he rearranged him a little, bending his knees and putting one hand under his head, as if he had fallen asleep there.

He gunned the car as he backed out of the street, then calmed down. He smiled at himself in the mirror. He had succeeded once more.

15

Three bad omens. She counted them. First, she stumbled over her slippers as she got out of bed, so she went to the bathroom in her bare feet. Then she stepped into the sand that Morty had scattered from his litter tray. Thirdly, once she got into the kitchen, her coffee machine refused to get going, so she would have to boil up a Greek coffee instead. Three signs of bad luck on a Tuesday – no doubt more would follow.

She opened the kitchen window and immediately regretted not putting her socks on. Radu would have brought them to her, if he'd been there. He was the only man she had ever actually moved in with, and she wondered why she kept thinking of him every morning. No doubt the joy of being rid of him, not any regrets. They had only been on holiday together once. The summer before this one, she had stayed at home on her own, to write and breathe, while he had gone to the seaside. Now she would have plenty of time to do all the writing and breathing she wanted. She couldn't help wondering if she had provoked him on purpose, to chase him away. She was pretty sure that she was glad to see the back of him: being too close to other human beings suffocated her somehow.

She had woken up from a bad dream. She couldn't remember exactly what, but something about walking down the street and hearing footsteps behind her.

After ransacking all her kitchen cupboards, she finally

managed to find the coffee grinder. It would have been a nightmare not to have it, she would have just stared at those coffee beans. Instead of waiting for the coffee to boil, she poured hot water over two heaped teaspoonfuls of ground coffee, as if it were instant. She poured a dash of milk over it. After one sip, she spat out the coffee grounds. But it was better than nothing, she supposed.

Today she would head to the police station and examine those boards again, in the hope that she might get some fresh ideas. At least the slenderest of threads.

It was cold and cloudy. If it started to rain at this time of the year it wouldn't stop for a week. She took out her phone to check the weather forecast: nine days of rain. Summer was over – and winter was never far behind autumn in Braşov. She realised her feet had automatically taken her to her workplace at the institute, so she turned around and headed for Ceasu Rău intersection, where the traffic was heaving. On the corner stood the eponymous restaurant, which had previously had the more innocuous name of Timiş. It had acquired its name of Ceasu Rău/Evil Hour because so many accidents seemed to take place at that intersection. Others said it was nonsense, the origin of the name was a clock at the entrance to the restaurant, which worked only occasionally. Two lovers had planned to meet there at six o'clock but never found each other again.

Gigi entered the police station and saw Matei laughing as he chatted to someone on the phone.

'Are you crazy? What reason do I have to arrest the guy who posted that online? It's not his fault. He wasn't leaking any info about a crime, because he didn't realise it was a crime. Oh, I see, the relatives are suing him... I see... Have a good day then!'

'Who was that?' asked Gigi, as Matei put the phone down.

'Good morning to you and thanks for the coffee,' he

raised it to his lips, 'Goodness, it's very hot.'

'I wish they'd write that on the lid,' Gigi agreed. 'So, what's the deal?'

'A worker who arrived on a building site this morning found a drunkard sleeping it off on the foundations of the house they were working on. He took a picture and posted it on Facebook, then, when he tried to wake the guy up, he realised he was dead. He called the police, they came and picked up the body, but the picture stayed on social media. And now people are complaining – because, as you know, it's illegal to publish pictures of corpses.'

'Here in Braşov?'

'No, in Bucharest. The post was quite amusing, of the type: "Look how hard we work here in Romania!" or "sleeping on the job" or something like that. The guy who posted it thought it was one of his workmates. It went viral quite quickly. Let's check the news, I'm sure there'll be a bit of a scandal about it.'

'You've got a TV here?'

'Of course I do.' He opened the wall cupboard and took out the remote.

The newsreader looked anxious and was slightly agitated as he talked about 'lack of humanity', while in the background they showed the images of the original Facebook post on a loop (with the face blurred out, however), and pictures of the house being built, from a distance, with a yellow police cordon around it, and crowds gathering to have a look, including a young man who kept trying to appear on camera showing a victory sign just behind the reporter.

'This is what happens when we are more concerned about our fifteen minutes of fame rather than showing some compassion for our fellow citizens. The police has been searching for the man who did this despicable deed but was unable to find him at home.'

'What, so now the poor guy who posted this is to blame?'

'Well, at least they know for sure who posted it,' Matei said.

'That's ridiculous, I can't believe it.'

'You'd better believe it, it's typical!' said Matei and switched off the TV.

The door opened wide and Tomescu walked in.

'That's all we needed, a media storm!'

'Morning, Vlad. Don't get so upset, it's nothing to do with us, it's not so bad,' said Gigi and handed him her latte.

Vlad collapsed into one of the chairs and gulped down his coffee noisily.

'Why are you so upset about it?' asked Gigi, pulling a chair to sit down next to him.

'It's like the Caracal case all over again. I hate it when journalists give out all sorts of details and create a panic.'

'That was a completely different situation. The Caracal girl could have been saved. In this case, the man was already dead. Did they mention where it took place?'

'They gave the exact address, those idiots, so a lot of the people living around there are milling around to take a look.'

'Really? Are they allowed to do that?' Gigi couldn't suppress a laugh.

'There will be an inquiry into what happened. The poor man's wife found out on Facebook that he was dead. The guy who posted it edited the post and then deleted it later.'

'And he's disappeared now?' asked Matei.

'So it seems. Or else the police is questioning him, which is far more likely. I don't want to phone them though. After all, we've got our own cases to worry about. Any news?'

'Nothing here,' sighed Matei, 'what about you?'

'Nope. Other than the exact chemical composition of the homemade explosive, which can be purchased just about anywhere.'

'You've said that before. Stop repeating yourself. In the meantime, I've been checking out the hairdresser's clients.

I thought maybe the guy who killed Irina Oprea had gone there to have his hair cut at some point, so someone might have seen him.'

'Have they finished checking all the CCTV recordings?'

'I don't know. We're a bit short-staffed, as you know. Vlad, can you really not spare us a couple more people?'

'No way. We're still taking statements from the hundred or more people who visited the exhibition. We've gathered all the pictures taken there. Two guys are creating a timeline and choosing the most relevant photos. It's a massive job. I haven't got a clue how much longer it will take.'

'Aren't the special forces helping?'

'They're just double checking whatever we are doing. In parallel. A waste of time, the idiots. At this rate, it'll take us a month. Here are some pictures of the exhibits. Nice, weren't they?'

Gigi took the pictures from Vlad and accidentally touched his hand. 'Ouch! You electrocuted me.'

'So there still is a spark between us,' Vlad whispered.

'Oy, lovebirds, don't act as if I weren't here!'

Gigi wondered if such a jokey exchange would have been possible a few months ago. They had been hiding from each other so much that they had generated a noxious atmosphere around them. The elephant in the room, the lie that was making her ill.

She stole a glance at Matei, then finally looked down at the photos. The spout of a zinc watering can was hanging crookedly from a metal rod, rusty at both ends. The rose was the head of a bird, the wings were made of long metal wires, grouped together to make it look like the bird was flying. Wavy metal fragments hung from each of the wires, resembling feathers. The body of the creature was covered in very thin layers of tin, some shiny and golden, others rusty, yet others glimmering silvery. Gigi put the picture down on the table and exclaimed: 'This is really beautiful!

If I had more space in my house, I wouldn't mind exhibiting that.'

'Yes, I quite liked some of them too. You should see the crow!'

'The crow?'

'Yes, it should be here somewhere.' Vlad bent over her to search for the picture. She could feel his minty breath. She looked down at her skirt, admiring the intricate, fine fabric print of colourful houses. She occupied herself by counting the windows in those houses until he managed to find the picture and hold it up.

'Here it is! What do you think?'

The crow was gigantic. Its body was composed of four garden spades, two pointing downwards, two pointing upwards The wings were fashioned out of multiple shovel blades, one on top of the other. The head was a sphere with tiny spikes all over. The eyes were metal beads, so shiny that you could have sworn they were looking straight at you. The beak was made of paper-thin knife blades, forming a svelte silvery pyramid without a single blemish.

'Is it a crow or a raven? Whatever it is, it's the only one he bothered to paint, because he couldn't find a spade black enough, yet still showing rust spots,' said Gigi, putting the pictures back on the table.

'Sure. But what I find interesting is that he kept taking pictures of the crow. It's an older piece of work but he never wanted to sell it. He's had it for over two years now, takes new pictures every month and posts things about it. He says that if it were alive, Gaspar – that's the name of the crow – would certainly have many things to tell us.'

'You've done your research,' said Matei, clapping slowly.

'I kinda liked the guy. Not just when questioning him, but what I read up on him. He's very careful in everything he does, a born storyteller. Gaspar is the name of one of the Three Wise Men. I think the artist was very upset to lose all his work like that. Otherwise, I might have been tempted to think he had a hand in the destruction. A hand... artist... get it?' Vlad was laughing but stopped when he saw that the others barely smiled in response. 'Well, I thought it was funny. Anyway, he didn't set the bomb.'

'Why would he? Just for the publicity?'

'Of course. The newspapers are full of him, he's been commissioned to recreate the pieces that were lost. Some art associations have already sent him money.'

'I see. Any enemies?'

'Money and enemies go hand in hand, right? Nothing out of the ordinary. The man simply went about his business, never caused any trouble, he's been in a stable relationship for the past five years with the guy who is also his official photographer...'

'A guy?' Matei, who had been completely silent up to that moment, raised his head from his computer screen.

'Yeah, he's a poofter.'

'Vlad, that's a horrible thing to say.'

'Ah, sorry, Gigi, I forgot you are so sensitive to minority needs...'

'Yes, I am. But you don't think this has anything to do with the attack on his art?'

'No. Where hate crime is involved, we usually get some warnings beforehand, or messages claiming responsibility afterwards. But nothing. We can't even accuse any ultra-nationalist sentiment in this case. The guy is easy-going, clean, without any issues.'

'So we need to look elsewhere? But where the hell?' Gigi thought out loud.

'I haven't got a clue. That's why I came to get you to think about it as well. If you like, come to my office and have a look at the panel I set up there, including all his travels around Europe.'

'I might drop by later, it sounds interesting and we've reached a bit of a dead end in our investigation anyway. But later, I've got to take this now,' Gigi picked up her phone and left the room.

It was an unknown number and normally she wouldn't have bothered to reply. But she needed an excuse to get out of that room. The truth was that being so close to Vlad wore her out. She was constantly testing her perceptions, second-guessing her feelings. She wasn't sure if he was deliberately trying to make her uncomfortable or repressing something himself.

'Morning, Gigi, it's Lucian Conrad. We met at the Urology Conference.'

'I remember. Hello, Lucian.'

'Could we meet up for a coffee?'

'I beg your pardon?'

'I've got a case I would like to consult you about.'

'Where did you get my mobile number from?'

'From one of your colleagues at work, Emil. I called your office first, of course.'

'And why do you want to meet up? I'm not currently working at the Institute, you could have asked Emil for help. He was the one who was supposed to be presenting at the conference, you might remember.'

'Yes, but I really would like to see you again. I hope you liked the tulips.'

'Ah, so you sent those? I asked everyone around here. Thank you for the flowers, but you could have signed your name.'

'I'm a bit shy. And then I kept thinking about you, so I finally got up my courage to call.'

'So there is no case you want to discuss?'

'There is, but it's not that exciting. Merely a kidney riddled with kidney stones and yet somehow still functioning.'

'I'm sorry, but I'm very busy right now.'

'If you are indeed sorry, maybe you can call me whenever you do have a spare moment and we could meet up when it suits you.'

'Fine. I'll bear that in mind. Thank you.'

'No, I thank you and have a good day.'

Out of the corner of her eye, she saw Matei coming out of the office. She hesitated, her hand hovering over the door handle, before she finally had the courage to press it down and open the door. Vlad was standing by the window.

'Shall we bury the hatchet once and for all?' he said.

'Is that why you sent Matei away?'

'He left of his own free will, I didn't say a word.'

'Sure he did. Expect me to believe that?'

'Yes!'

Gigi sat down abruptly, 'I'm so tired.'

'Let's go out for dinner tonight.'

He came up closer and squatted on his haunches right next to her. He looked in her eyes and she could feel her heart rate increasing. She didn't have the time to snatch her arm away from the armrest, and winced when he touched it.

'No. You're asking for too much. I know you said we were just friends. We had the exact same discussion before you left for Bucharest, you might remember. This just won't work! I need more time, and I just can't trust you.'

She fixed her eyes on a spot on his neck. The smell of him still seemed to activate a very sensitive part of her brain. She could feel her breasts getting heavier, and she had to clench her thighs.

'Stop it, Vlad! It's too pathetic to start it all up again.'

'I felt a slight tremor, you know.'

'And I can feel your erection even at a distance. So what! That doesn't stop me from saying enough is enough. We are not going to start this all over again. I've had enough of cheap melodrama.'

'But it could be different this time...'

'Please stand up. If someone comes in and finds you kneeling here in front of me...'

'We could just meet up occasionally...'

'For a fuck, you mean?'

He stood up and walked up to the window once more.

'Don't talk like that. I merely meant we could enjoy spending some time together.'

'Listen very carefully, because I hate repeating myself. Although I can foresee I might have to in this instance, because you just can't take no for an answer. There will never be anything between us, even if my body still yearns for your dick.'

'Gigi!'

'Oh, stop being so sensitive about my language, Vlad! That's the truth and you know it. You can use your charms and influence on someone else, because I'm not frightened of you. I will leave now, but please remember the most salient points of this conversation. And in actual fact, you should be the one leaving, because this is my office.'

Vlad left the room without another word. She gave a deep sigh of relief. She searched for the last call on her phone and tapped her fingers on the table until someone answered.

'Hello, Lucian, it's Gigi.'

'Hello, I hope you're calling to say that you've changed your mind.'

'I have indeed I've got an hour off in two hours' time. Want to go for a coffee? Somewhere nearby, if you can.'

'Certainly. Where?'

'There's a coffee shop just opposite the police station, called Zuze. Let's meet there.'

'What on earth is Zuze?'

'High-spirited, feisty girls, something like that.'

'OK, we'll search for those girls at around two o'clock. Is that OK?'

'Yes, thanks.'

When Matei rejoined her, she was standing by the boards.

'Have you cleared the air?'

'What are you getting at, Matei?'

'There was such tension between the two of you that I preferred to stay out of it. You can tell me if there's anything to tell.'

'I simply clarified my position.'

'You mean?'

'That I have no wish to see him again.'

'Are you sure about that?'

'Absolutely certain. I have to admit that my heart does skip a beat when he comes near me, but that's just muscle memory, no need to make a drama out of it. Honestly, we all take ourselves far too seriously.'

'Listen, I'm kind of your manager here. I know it might sound bizarre to say it, but let's be clear... if you feel that he is pushing or harassing you, you need to let me know.'

Gigi gave a deep sigh, and held out her hand to Matei: 'It's a deal, boss.'

'Don't you dare make fun of me.'

'I'm not. Honestly, I think you're cool and I admire you for that. And very brave. I know that here in our country people don't really talk about such things, but it's honestly not the case now between me and Vlad. It's all been resolved. Or rather, I should say that even if he is still trying to win me over, I don't feel under any kind of pressure. But I do appreciate your openness. By the way, if we stay on the subject, I'd like to suggest something for you too.'

'Since when are you so polite as to ask for permission?'

'It happens on occasion. Just wanted to say it would be best if you announced officially that you are going out with Alina.'

'I've already done that.'

'Really?'

'Yes, I sent a memo to Bucharest a couple of months after we became a couple.'

'And they gave you their blessing?'

'Stop teasing! They thanked me for letting them know.' Matei noticed that Gigi was stuffing things into her handbag once more. 'Are you going out?'

'For a coffee.'

'Again?'

'I've only had three today.'

'Who with?'

'Aren't you being a bit indiscreet?'

'No. Is it Radu?'

'No, we broke up. I'm having a coffee with a urologist who wants to discuss a case with me.'

'So that's why you're putting on lipstick?'

'Obviously. Since I'm not going to be kissing him.'

'Ha, funny joke. So I should take it that only women with no lipstick on want to be kissed?'

'Stop analysing everything I do!'

'OK, tell me about him when you get back.'

'I know you're just teasing, so I'll pretend I didn't hear that.'

**

Gigi smiled as she walked down the stairs. The only reason she had acquiesced to meeting with Lucian was because having another man in her life would help to keep any thoughts of Vlad firmly out of her head. She was sick and tired of the pattern she and Vlad had fallen into. She would say that they could no longer see each other, then they had a long professional meeting or collaborated on some important project, then she would give in to that sense of ease and comfort, the feeling that he understood and validated her. Strange that she should need precisely those things from him that he couldn't give her. She had often reproached herself for not being more casual about things, simply enjoying their occasional hook-ups. She also reproached herself for wanting something more from him. She knew all that in theory, but in practice... it was hard to be your own shrink.

If only she'd had a different analyst than Fora, maybe she would have been able to overcome her insecurities. True, Fora had helped her during those awful high school years, treating her as an equal, allowing her to grow and develop. There had been just one mis-step, and that was when she stopped trusting him. She had told him about her anger, and that she needed to find a scapegoat. She couldn't blame her mother for leaving her behind without any letter or explanation. But she could blame her father for being cold and distant with her mother, for driving her to drink. And Fora had fanned the flames of her desire for revenge a little too much.

Nevertheless, she still had long conversations with Fora in her head when she was unsure what to do next. She could hear him now, scolding her for going out to see someone new, instead of trying to repair things with Radu. It was certainly not the urology case study that was making her go out to meet him. Lucian himself had admitted that was a mere pretext. However, she was sick and tired of pretending that things were OK in her relationship with Radu. His neediness and jealousy drove her mad. She should have made more of an effort to understand and reassure him, but it had all got too much for her. Then, to top it all, he forgot her birthday...

She was still smiling as she crossed the road. The café had opened up recently, but she had never been inside.

'You should fix these steps,' were Gigi's first words as she entered the coffee shop.

'We certainly will! How can I help? Do you want to try one of our specialist teas?'

'Just a latte, please. Do you have a courtyard as well?'

'Yes, out through the second room.'

The atmosphere was that of a youthful, cosy living room in someone's house: orange sofa, purple and burgundy chairs, brightly-coloured paintings. A bit tiring on the eye, but warm and pleasant enough. She nearly burst out laughing when she saw a kitschy glass fish on one of the table, that ubiquitous piece of art during Communist times. It wasn't that ugly in and of itself – it had been copied after a Murano model, after all – but its simplification and mass production had made it synonymous with bad taste. She wondered if the decorators had been feeling nostalgic or simply had a wicked sense of humour.

The courtyard was lovely however. Although you could still hear a little of the street noise, the outside world seemed far removed from here. Lucian was sitting at a table in the shade and stood up when he saw her. He had looked very fit in his suit at the conference, but now he looked even better, in jeans and a simple T-shirt. He appeared to be tanned and well-rested. His hair was slightly longer than when she had first seen him. He gave her a hearty smile.

'Hi, Gigi, so pleased you agreed to meet.'

'Hi, nice to see you are so punctual. I thought I was arriving two minutes early.' She held out her hand, and Lucian kissed it, which made her giggle.

'Don't you think that's a bit old-fashioned?'

'Maybe,' was all he said, as he pulled back the chair so she could sit down.

'Have you been on holiday? You look quite tanned.'

'I took a week off. Just pottered around the house and went for short hikes, but I needed a break.'

'Well, it suits you,' said Gigi. She felt slightly uncomfortable with the way he kept staring at her.

'Thank you for the compliment. Have you already ordered? I would have done it, but I wasn't sure what you wanted to drink. They've got an astounding collection of teas as well...'

'I asked for a latte and told them to bring it out here. It's a nice place, very cheerful.'

'That's what I thought. And I'm glad it's just the two of us...' Lucian stopped suddenly when the waitress brought the coffee for Gigi.

'Would you like anything else? We have some fresh brioches...'

'No, thanks,' he said hurriedly, then stopped to check with Gigi. She shook her head as well. 'Maybe just some water, please.'

'Certainly. We also have lemonade with mint, if you prefer...'

'No, water is fine.'

The young waitress finally left.

'As I was saying, I was really looking forward to seeing you again. I've often thought about you.'

'You weren't saying any of that. You just made it up now,' Gigi laughed. 'Isn't this all a bit sudden?'

'Not at all. You are absolutely fabulous!'

'Wow, Lucian, you're a fast mover! Anyway, what about that case you wanted to discuss with me?'

'I told you it was just a pretext, so what would have been the point in bringing it along?'

'You're not wrong there. So tell me about yourself.'

'There's nothing much to tell. I'm a very boring person and I'm a bit bored of this town. I've been thinking of moving back to Bucharest, but something is keeping me here. The mountains, the forests, I like going jogging on the Tâmpa.'

'You take the cable car?'

'No, I take the car to the lower path, leave it there and then sprint up the hill. It takes me about half an hour to the top and another half hour back. Ideal for keeping fit. I do that four times a week: Monday, Wednesday, Friday and Saturday.'

'Do you plan everything in your life?'

'Not quite,' Lucian smiled. 'For example, I wanted to ask you out, but didn't quite dare to do it until today. No, it's more like I need to keep busy.'

'You mean by meeting up with me?'

'No, I mean with running. I need to feel that I've got something to do every day, otherwise I'd go mad.'

'When did you move here?'

'Just over a year ago.'

'May I ask why?'

'Of course you may. I think city life in Bucharest was getting to me. I lived in Germany for six years, just outside Frankfurt. I was working for a clinic on the outskirts of the city and I lived in a village nearby. It was very quiet. Almost too quiet. Which is why I came back to Romania in 2015. But then Bucharest got to be too overwhelming. Hard to find the balance, right? What about you, are you from here?'

'Yes, and I've always lived here, with the exception of my student years in Cluj.'

'So you must like this place.'

'There are too many ties that bind me to it. And I can't complain, I have sufficient things to keep me busy professionally.'

'I heard that you collaborate with the police. How come?'

'I'm the BAU, not the boo!' She saw him looking puzzled and explained: 'Sorry, that was my attempt at a pun. The BAU is the Behavioural Analysis Unit, which is actually based in Bucharest, but I contributed to a major case here a year ago and so they got me to collaborate with them on a regular basis.'

'So you're a sort of detective?'

'Not really. There isn't a name for what I do. I merely observe and point out certain things and they seem to rely on me more and more.'

'Do you like it?'

Yes, it's fascinating. I'm always keen to understand more.'

'And what are you working on now?'

'Some quite complicated cases, actually.'

'Really? I thought this was the dullest town in Romania.'

'Oh, you're exaggerating. Although I might have said something similar in the past. I guess that places like Turda or Baia Mare might be even duller? No, I know what you mean, and to be honest, I did find it a bit too quiet when I returned from Cluj. But my work is very important to me, so I like it here. I suppose you're the same.'

'Work is work. I don't have a higher purpose like you.'

'Ah, what is my higher purpose then?'

'Oh, you are good at questioning, you've certainly learnt something from the police!' Lucian laughed.

'That's exactly what my colleagues say, and I don't think they mean that as a compliment!'

'So what are those complicated cases you're working on now?'

'They've been all over the papers. Haven't you read about them?'

'I don't really read the papers. I don't even have a TV. Anyway, I doubt any of them made it on the national news.'

'Actually, one of them did. An explosion in an art gallery. They think it might have been a terrorist attack, so there was quite a lot of speculation about that.'

'Really? Where? When?'

'A week ago.'

'I must have been away at the time. What happened?'

'It was a home-made bomb. Luckily, it exploded overnight, so only material damage. A gallery on Mureşenilor.'

'I don't often come into the town centre. I go running straight after my shift at the hospital. And on the days when I don't run, I often have private surgery hours in the afternoon. That's why I can't stay any longer now, I start work at three. I merely wanted to see you, however briefly.'

'I'm glad we got to see each other. That was quite funny about the flowers.'

'Sorry, I didn't mean to cause you any distress, I thought it was a fun little game, a surprise.'

'You didn't send me some wine, by any chance?'

'No. What wine?' He looked surprised.

'Never mind.'

'Would you like to have dinner with me tonight?' He bent over and took her hand.

She pulled it back almost instantly. 'I told you I was busy.'

'Yes, I know. You said. I was hoping you might have changed your mind.'

'Let's wait for things to calm down. I don't even know what time I'll get home in the evening.'

'I understand. But maybe later, after you finish work. We could go the Belvedere Restaurant, on the way to Poiana Braşov. If it's not raining, we could sit out on the terrace.'

'I don't think I can.'

'If not tonight, maybe one of the following evenings?'

'We'll see. I'll keep in touch. I need to go back, it's been nearly an hour. I told them I'd only be out for half an hour.'

'OK, then, let's talk again later. I'll pay for the coffee. Please do have a think about going out with me again. I'll certainly be thinking of you.'

They both stood up and he took a step towards her. She quickly held her hand out, to avoid any hugs. He froze, let his arms drop helplessly by his side for a moment, then took her hand and once again raised it to his lips, almost by force.

'See you later, my beauty.'

'Yes, fine. Bye '

She turned quickly and kept her head down while she left through the front. She nearly stumbled over the front steps once more and swore under her breath. She felt hounded and crossed the street without looking, just hearing the squeal of brakes as cars stopped suddenly. He had been very unsubtle, very insistent. He was just a stranger after all. This invitation to dinner out of the blue... this almost aggressive way of greeting her or saying goodbye ... is that how men were, nowadays? Were her social skills all awry?

She met Vlad just outside Matei's office.

'What have you been up to?'

'I beg your pardon?'

'I merely asked where you've been, no need to be offended.'

'I went out for a coffee.'

'OK. Here, I found something. Let's discuss it with Matei too.'

Vlad opened the door and let her go through first. He followed a little too closely behind her, as if sniffing her scent. She turned to face him suddenly, and he nearly fell over her.

'What are you doing? Get in!'

'Stop squabbling, you two,' said Matei, looking up from his computer.

'I've spoken to the colleagues from Bucharest and they checked the registrations of all the cars spotted on Călușei Street and you'll never guess...'

'They found something?'

'One of the cars had the number plate covered with reflective foil. So it seems to have been something premeditated.'

'You mean the guy they found on the building site?'

'Yes, and he was poisoned with cyanide, not just drunk.'

'And why are you telling us?' asked Gigi.

'I thought you might be interested. It's nothing to do with our case, I know, but a nice little detail anyway.'

'I've discovered something too,' muttered Matei.

'You have?'

'Yes.' Matei rolled his eyes dramatically. 'I've discovered we're in deeep shit!'

Gigi pretended to slap him on the head. 'Come on, Matei, stop kidding around!'

'Honestly, Gigi, I keep thinking we must be missing something. Better go through everything again. But first, I need a piss.' Matei left the office scowling.

Vlad immediately jumped in. 'Want to go out for dinner with me tonight?'

'What the hell is wrong with you all? Did you not hear me say no earlier?'

'What do you mean, with us all?'

'Never mind. But I told you quite clearly that we cannot be good friends.'

'Why not?'

'Let's just drop this subject, Vlad, please.'

'If you wish.'

When Matei got back to the office, Gigi was alone.

'Lovers' tiff?'

'Stop laughing at me, Matei. Let's check out those damn noticeboards again, see if we get any new ideas.'

16

The Eighth

She drew the curtain gently aside to look out on the street. She thought she had heard a car and she was glad to see some movement outside, even though it was late and no one ever came to visit her anyway. She had been home from hospital for over a month now. She put her hand up to the cavernous waste on her chest, and felt a renewed sense of vertigo at the thought of what was missing. They had assured her that she would get reconstructive surgery soon, but she had to wait for the wound to heal, and finish the course of chemotherapy she was about to embark upon. They had reluctantly allowed her to take a break, although they had initially advised her to start chemo immediately. But she just hadn't had the strength.

She struggled to admit even to herself how much this mutilation had changed her. Yes, she did think of it as a sort of mutilation. The cancer itself had been nearly invisible, a tiny lump she had discovered one evening after a lengthy bath. She had been drying herself with her towel when she thought she felt something hard in her right breast. She took some cream to do a more thorough check in front of the fogged-up bathroom mirror. She wiped the mirror with the palm of her hand, but it was still fuzzy, so she scrubbed it with her towel, then lifted her arm high above her head and searched for the nodule. It was there, she had been right. She waited for two days, continued going to school as if nothing had happened. She made a doctor's appointment during the holidays. She knew that she might be away for some time and she wanted to avoid any gossip. Even her best friends – she only let them know once she had a date for the operation, and she only spoke to them on the phone. She preferred not to see them. She could hear the worry in their voices, but she pretended to be brave. She let them visit her only after she got out of hospital, all on the same day, knowing that it would be easier to keep up appearances that way. They too would have to pretend all was well if there were other people present. They too would have to deal with their own fears, aside from their anxiety about her wellbeing.

The only person visiting her every morning was the nurse, injecting her with vitamins and anti-inflammatories. She couldn't bear to swallow them, and besides her stomach was starting to hurt. She also had to look after the incision, now the bandages had come off. After two weeks, it seemed fairly clean. She had just been at the hospital yesterday to have the stitches removed and they'd told her it was all healing well, she would only have a minor scar. But she could still feel the void, no matter how much reconstruction she might have in the future.

She heard the doorbell and cast an anxious glance at the clock above the fireplace. Ten at night – who on earth could it be so late? She went to the hallway and pressed the intercom button.

'Who is it?'

'Good evening. I'm your neighbour from the next road over, from Codrul Cosminului street. I am very sorry to disturb you, but my boys were playing football and the ball went into your garden. I hope you don't mind. I saw the light was still on and thought it might be all right to ring.'

'I'll come down and open the door. But will you be able to find it?'

'I'll try,' the man laughed.

'Can I help?'

'That's kind of you. I do have a torch, but maybe you can have a look as well?'

When she went out into the front yard, he was standing at the gate holding a rose bouquet.

'Please accept these as a small thank you, with my apologies for disturbing you. I cut them from my own garden. My little scoundrels begged me to come for the ball tonight, they didn't want to wait until morning.'

'Thank you, they are beautiful,' she took the roses, lowering her head to take in the scent. 'They smell delicious, like marmalade.'

'Please take care, they are full of thorns. That's why I didn't take my gloves off, and why I hold them at a slight distance. I don't know what type of roses they are, I just look after them. I inherited them when I bought the house.'

'Have you moved here recently? Let me switch on another light.'

'No need, I have the torch on my phone. I'll start searching, you go and put the flowers in water.'

'Yes. I'll be right back.'

The lights were off in the kitchen, she carefully moved the roses to her left hand so she could switch on the light. She felt him standing behind her. She turned around, surprised, about to ask him what he was looking for, but the man grabbed her suddenly, whirled her round and stifled her cry, so that it came out more like a whimper. She tried to fight back, but the strength ebbed out of her. Her last thought was that she had left the gate open.

17

When Gigi opened her eyes, it was dark. She lay still for a moment, listening to the sound of the rain. She saw the lightning, a prolonged series of flashes. She held her breath and started counting the seconds, like her father had taught her when she was a child, so that she could calculate her distance from the eye of the storm. The clap of thunder came after less than five seconds and shook the entire house. She stretched out in bed and checked her phone. It was six in the morning, she might as well get up, there was no way she could fall asleep again with that noise.

She searched for her slippers next to the bed. When she put them on, she felt one of her toes poking out of the slipper on her right foot. She loved those slippers beyond any reason, but she knew she might have to say goodbye to them soon. There had simply been too many goodbyes lately. She almost burst out laughing, typical nervous response to stress.

She and Matei had stayed up until two in the morning, going over all the details again, checking all the information they held on the two women, but they still couldn't find any common denominator: school, residential addresses, social circle, their paths had never crossed. They would start over again this morning, go over all the witness statements.

Lucian had sent her a message last night: 'Braşov is even more beautiful by night. I would have liked to have you here with me.' She reread the message several times but decided not to reply. What could she have said? That she was regretting the impulse to go for a coffee with him? That she didn't quite know what to make of him? That she was somewhat attracted to him? It was too soon to go into any details and she was too busy to engage in meaningless chit-chat.

Lucian was a very good-looking man, but there was something about him that didn't sit well with her. He was too sleek, too perfect, with his side parting, the way he shook his head to get his hair out of his eyes, a bit like a stallion, his manicured fingernails, which were in better condition than her own. He clearly knew how to look after himself, unlike her. She had never had a manicure in her life, she considered it a waste of time. As for the hairdresser... well, let's just say she was lucky to have naturally curly hair, so that she could get away with cutting it twice a year. She had never followed fashion, not even when everyone was straightening their hair. She didn't have to dye her hair yet either, the few grey hairs she had were almost hidden in her blonde mop.

She was on her second cigarette of the day as she went through her emails. Matei was constantly surprised that she refused to waste her time on social media. But she was too wary of creating a profile and allowing friends and acquaintances to find her there. Too many ghosts of the past. She knew it was not quite normal perhaps, but she didn't care about that.

The reply from the University of Groningen saddened her. They had postponed her application for the spring. Of course they had, they weren't going to make an exception in her case, and besides, she had been unable to get all the paperwork together by the 15th of September. Anyway, she wouldn't have been able to leave in the middle of a case.

She was still not sure if they were dealing with a single case or two unrelated ones. She found it hard to believe that there could suddenly be two murderers in town. Rumour had it that Braşov was the town with the highest number of violent crimes, but she had never checked the statistics too closely. She was pretty sure that Bucharest must have more crimes, but maybe they were counting them in proportion to the number of inhabitants. She would have to do some research, she hated leaving any questions unanswered.

She was about to head to the shower when her phone started vibrating.

'Hello, Matei. So you didn't sleep well either?'

'Gigi, it's getting serious!'

'What do you mean?'

'We've got another gruesome crime. I'll come and get you in ten minutes.'

'What? Where?'

'We had a phone call. The victim is a woman living by herself, her throat's been cut. Get dressed, I'll come and get you. You weren't asleep, were you?'

'No, I slept badly.'

'It's cold, by the way. Winter's on its way.'

When he arrived, Matei looked like he hadn't slept in days. He seemed to have aged suddenly overnight.

'Have you been there? What's with this woman?'

'I passed by and let the forensic team get on with things. It's sheer butchery,' Matei said, careful to avoid her eyes. 'I've honestly never seen anything like it.'

Gigi decided to keep silent. The rain was lashing down, the windscreen wipers were powerless. They parked the car on Vulcan, behind the church, just as the bells started ringing.

'Is it a holiday today? Why are they ringing?'

'How do you expect me to know? I think it's on the hour. Seven o'clock.'

The gate was wide open, as was the door to the house. They put on their protective suits.

'Where are your pink gloves?'

'I forgot them at home. I've got a box of them, but I keep forgetting to take them with me.'

'I for one am glad you forgot them. I find them quite distracting. Take these everyday ones.'

She pulled on her gloves and adjusted them as they entered the front room. Everything seemed intact there. A woman was sitting on an armchair, bent slightly forward, with her hands resting on her knees. She was soaked through, with water pooling all around her.

'This is the nurse who came in early this morning. She had keys. The lady was undergoing treatment.'

Gigi sensed the smell as soon as she entered the bedroom. That sickly sweet, slightly sour, warm smell. Her stomach lurched, but she took a deep breath and stepped forward. The woman was lying on her back on the bed. Her eyes were closed, her hands folded across her chest as if she was laid out at a mortuary. Gigi took another step forward, sniffed the air, but the smell of blood was too strong, she could feel the nausea rising in her throat. She turned to face the wall, leaning on it, doing her best to stay upright, breathing in and out. Slowly, slowly, in and out. She tried to identify any other smells: washing powder, fabric softener – the bedsheets had been recently changed. The smell of an old, damp house. Something sweet. A perfume? No, sweeter than that. Chloroform.

'Search for a cloth with chloroform,' said Gigi, still facing the wall.

'We found one on the bedside table on the other side. We haven't lifted her yet,' replied the crime scene officer.

'OK. Let me turn around and take a look at her.'

'You're not feeling well,' Matei, concerned, put a hand on her shoulder.

'Nauseous.'

'I thought you were made of steel.'

'I've never been able to bear the smell of fresh blood.'

'I thought you were immune to anything to do with dead bodies...'

'By the time they come to me, they are less fresh. I've only recently started attending a crime scene.'

'And this really is a horrible scene. Are you ready?'

'Yes,' Gigi braced herself and turned to look at the bed.

The woman was completely naked, posed in the centre of the double bed. The gash on her throat was so deep, that it looked like the wide-open mouth of some creature. The blood had not dried completely, the bedsheet was soaked. She must have been cut right there, the killer must have watched the blood flow out.

'Please take samples from the bedsheets. He must have sat down on the bed,' said Gigi.

'How do you know?' asked Matei.

'There's too much blood on either side, but the incision is relatively clean. He must have moved her head from side to side to get as much blood out as possible. Maybe pressed on the wound. He cut slowly, there is no blood spatter. Have you finished? I would like to check something, move her arms.'

'Yes,' said a voice from beneath a mask. She thought it sounded familiar.

'I'm Mircea Vasile, we met before.'

'Ah, yes, sorry I didn't recognise you.'

'There are no fibres. He must have put something down on the bedsheet. You can move her, we're finished here.'

Gigi knelt down by the side of the bed and bent over the body. She gently took first the left arm and then the right arm and lifted them up. She started when she saw the flat chest and scar.

'She's had her right breast removed. Has anyone spoken to the lady who called the police?'

'We've not had time to exchange more than a few words. She said she came every morning to give her some injections. She is a nurse and a friend of the deceased,

Claudia Moraru.'

'May I speak to her?'

'Sure.'

She stepped away with care, as if not to wake up the victim. There was no sound, the protective slippers muffled everything. She pulled up a chair to sit down next to the nurse.

'Good morning,' Gigi tried to start the conversation, but all she could hear were the woman's sobs. 'I'm Dr Gigi Alexa, forensic pathologist assigned to the case. I am very sorry for your loss. Can I ask you who you are and what you did exactly since entering the house?'

The woman continued to hold her head in her hands and whispered, 'I'm a nurse. My name is Loredana Popa. Claudia and I are... were friends.'

Gigi did not jump in to intervene in the long silence that followed.

'I got here at six-thirty, like I usually do. I come here every morning before going to the hospital. I work at the neurology department, I'm a ward sister. I work the early shift this week. When I work the late shift, I pass by at seven in the morning. I never sleep late, so I don't mind. We have our coffee together. Or used to. I'm devastated. I don't understand. I had such a shock when I came in today. I called her from the hallway, while taking off my shoes and fighting to close my umbrella. I couldn't hear her, so I thought she might be asleep. I was hoping she'd get some sleep, she's been struggling with insomnia lately. She didn't want any morphine, so I just gave her some injectable ketoprofen, a small dose, plus some vitamins. And I would bathe her wound since they took off the bandages.'

'Please continue,' said Gigi, giving the woman her full attention.

'I went into the bedroom and saw her lying there, in the light coming in from the street. The curtains weren't drawn. I thought she was asleep. Luckily, I didn't get any closer. I switched on the light, although I didn't really want to wake her. But I had to, because I had to get to work. When I saw her like that, I just froze. I couldn't even scream. I couldn't process what I was seeing there. Then I started shaking like a leaf, took out my phone and called 112. I waited outside in the yard. Forgot my umbrella.'

'I understand you have a set of keys.'

'Yes, Claudia gave me a set, so I could get in and call for help in an emergency.'

'She lived on her own, Ms Moraru? Was she married, did she have a housemate?'

'No. That's why she gave me the keys, she had no one else to rely on.'

'When did you start coming in daily?'

'The last few weeks, since her operation. At first I came in the evening as well, she took some antibiotics. But more recently in the mornings only.'

'Did she have any other visitors?'

'Not that I know of. She did her shopping online and got it delivered. Since she came out of hospital, she barely left the house, only went out into the garden.'

'Does she have any relatives?'

'Not in Brașov. She has two older cousins in Bucharest. She hasn't got anyone here except her friends. She was a teacher, a Romanian language teacher.'

'Did her friends come to visit?'

'No, she didn't want them to. She invited them only once. I was supposed to join them, but I was on shift then. But she told me she didn't keep them long and sent them home.'

'Did she have a partner, boyfriend?'

'I told you she didn't,' Loredana finally raised her eyes and Gigi saw they were red and swollen with tears and rubbing.

'I am so sorry.'

The nurse gasped, and after a long pause, filled with a few silent sobs, she said, 'That's all right. Can I go now?'

'Yes. We'll ask you to come to the police station for a formal statement, and if you could let the relatives know that they need to handle some paperwork.'

'They're elderly. I'll maybe ask them for a power of attorney and solve things myself. They will come to the funeral of course.'

'Of course. Can I help you at all? Shall I ask someone to accompany you home?'

'I need to get to the hospital.'

'Maybe you should stay home today. Would you like me to let them know?'

'No, I can call my colleagues. They've already called me twice, but I didn't know what to tell them.'

'Would you like my number? Just in case?'

The woman's hands were trembling so much, she struggled to type in Gigi's number.

'Thanks.'

'Thank you and take good care of yourself.'

Gigi tried to help her up. She looked around for Nicu but couldn't see him.

'Nicu, Nicu, are you here?'

'Yes, Gigi,' he rushed into the room.

'Can you please drive Ms Popa home? She will give you her address, please check that she is all right. Ms Popa, is there someone who can stay with you at home?'

'Yes, my husband. He's not working today.'

'Do you want to check that he's there? Shall we call him?'

'No need. He's definitely home and resting, in this weather.'

'Nicu, please make sure that you leave her safely with Mr Popa. If he's not at home, please stay with her until he's back. Is that OK?'

'Absolutely, as you wish,' said Nicu.

**

She asked Matei to drop her in the town centre. It was nearly nine o'clock and things were starting to wake up in the Town Hall Square. He argued that they had work to do, that she should really be there at the autopsy, but she was adamant that she needed a bit of fresh air, to see things from a different angle. So he left her in peace, merely told her to show up for the meeting at three, when they got the preliminary results from the autopsy. She would have to talk to one of her colleagues and arrange for it to be prioritised.

She called Emil, who listened patiently to her mumbling, and only complained once that she was leaving all the hard work to them. She let him have his grumble and arranged for an immediate autopsy. After that, she felt like switching off her phone, but she knew she couldn't afford to do that as a police collaborator.

She sat down on the bench next to the fountain that never worked. Or rather, it had worked one single day a few years back, during another heavy rain. The whole town had laughed at the authorities, some had got upset or made any number of political comments. Far easier to imagine a conspiracy rather than accept bumbling incompetence as an explanation.

She tried to take in everything around her. She could feel the fat raindrops falling on her, listen to the splash they made when they hit her raincoat. She hated umbrellas: as a child she had always struggled with them in the wind. The only umbrella she would have accepted would have been one that allowed her to fly, but she had always been a realist. She'd never believed in Mary Poppins or Peter Pan or even Santa.

Her hair was tied back and she could feel a cold breeze at the back of her neck. The cold, wet bench was not particularly comfortable, but her feet were not soaked yet, so she could hold out for a little longer. She would have liked to smoke a cigarette. This was potentially the only time when an umbrella might have come in handy, but with the rain drumming on her raincoat it was impossible. She preferred to sit and observe things anyway. She liked the smell of the wet flagstones, and the dust being washed away. She could see bloodstains... She shook her head and they disappeared. Her imagination, as usual. She let the raindrops fall on her hands, enjoyed the sensation on each hand in turn, then shook them, stood up and went to the art gallery on Mureşenilor, since she was there anyway. There were still police cordons in place and an opaque foil cover replaced the windows.

Three women. That was the one thing they had in common. One had long curly blonde hair, the other black braids, the third short hair. None of them very young, but not old either. All three of them had lived on their own. No children. Irina Oprea did have a son, but he was an adult.

Gigi couldn't resist the smell rising from the kürtőskalác stand. She bought one of the chimney-shaped pastries covered in walnut and started nibbling at it then and there. The caramelised sugar stuck to her teeth and she tried to scrape it off. But she had forgotten to wash her hands after taking off her latex gloves, so the combined taste of talcum powder and dust made her spit out the food. She raised her face towards the sky and let the rain pour into her mouth to wash away the unpleasant taste.

Then she walked down Republicii as if she were a tourist. She checked out the buildings, glanced at the statues, but allowed her thoughts to roam free. As she got to the Modarom building, the most popular meeting place in the city, she heard her phone ringing. She didn't want to answer directly with her earbuds on, she wanted to see who it was first. She managed to locate her phone in one of the side pockets. The screen said: Chief Tomescu.

'Where the hell are you?'

'On Republicii. Why? Good morning to you too.'

'Come to the meeting.'

'Matei said it was at three. I've got plenty of time. What's the time now? Hang on, I can check for myself, but oh... the screen is blocked, plus I'm wet and I'm also holding a kürtős...'

'It's eleven. I'll send a car for you. If I can't find anyone, I'll fetch you myself. We have to come up with something or the Bucharest folk will be all over us.'

'Are you referring to the bomb or the murders?'

'Both. They're piling the pressure onto me.'

'Ooops. Fine. I'll stay put. Get them to give me a call when they are nearby, so I can sit under this overhanging roof and smoke a cigarette.'

'I'll be there in ten minutes.'

'You?'

'Yes. Do you think I don't need fresh air as well? I know what you are up to. The best ideas come when you try to disengage and see things afresh.'

'OK, we can discuss this in the car. Right now I can't take my cigarettes out if I'm holding the phone.'

'Don't you have your earbuds on?'

'Of course I do, as usual. Speak to you later.'

She shook her head in disbelief. She had been able to have a nearly normal conversation with him.

Gigi was almost glad that he was the one who came to pick her up and see her in that dishevelled state.

'Do you want to go home and change? You look wet. The water has dripped down your raincoat and your jeans are soaked.'

'Why, are you upset that I've got your car seat wet?'

'No need to be so abrasive. I merely thought you might want to get changed because we have a long day ahead, who knows when we'll be out of there.'

Gigi nodded, but said nothing further until he stopped outside her house.

'Hurry, I'll be waiting here.'

She was relieved that he remained outside. Morty came meowing up to her and she realised she had forgotten to feed him in the morning, so the first thing she did was go to the kitchen and prepare his meal. She glanced out of the window. The car had mounted the kerb right underneath the window. He couldn't see her from behind the curtain, and anyway, he appeared far too absorbed in checking his phone, possibly all hell had broken loose again.

She went into the bedroom, took off her wet clothes and simply left them in a pile on the floor. Even her feet were soaked. She would have loved to take a shower, her teeth were chattering. She checked the thermostat, but the temperature was not that low. She must have simply stayed in her damp clothes too long. She hurriedly put on a yellow T-shirt and a bulky jumper with geometrical patterns, as well as a pair of wide-legged velvet trousers. She opened several shoeboxes searching for her purple boots, to match the trousers, and resolved in future to write on each box what was inside.

She was back at the car in no more than five minutes.

'I'm fast, aren't I?'

'You are. Well done and thank you, let's see what's happening.'

**

Gigi went straight to the small meeting room where the noticeboards were set up. Claudia Moraru's picture had been added to them. She stretched out on the beanbag and examined all three panels closely. Three entirely unconnected women. Two strangled, one by hand, one with apron strings. One cut up. Chloroform had been used twice. There was no discernible pattern, but there must be a logic there somewhere. She closed her eyes, but jumped up when Vlad and Matei entered the room.

'We have to go to the big meeting room,' she told them.

'But that's where the bomb case is set out,' Vlad protested.

'They're linked.'

'How? What possible connection could there be?'

'Listen, I'll explain it to you first, and then in an hour we can let everyone else know. Let me put everything in order.'

'What do you mean?' asked Matei.

Gigi got up from her beanbag and invited them to sit down on the two chairs next to her.

'You know the story of Hercules?'

'What the...?' Vlad burst out.

'Hercules or Heracles was a hero and demi-god. His father was Zeus and...'

'For heaven's sake, Gigi, haven't you got anything better to do than tell us a story about the creation of the world or what?' Matei interrupted her.

'If you would shut up for just a few minutes, I can explain my idea. Since it's the only theory we have for the time being, don't you think it's worth a try?'

'Ok, go ahead, you have ten minutes,' said Vlad.

'So Hercules is the son of Zeus and a mortal woman. He is set twelve tasks or so-called labours to complete. Yes, I'm getting to the point, don't look at me like that. Do you know what those twelve labours were?' They shook their heads and frowned.

'OK, let me give you a potted summary. I had to remind myself briefly and check it out on the phone too. First was the Nemean Lion – the Lion took on the shape of a woman to attract its victims.'

'Are you referring to Andrada Vasiliu?' Matei said, getting up from his chair. Gigi pointed at him to sit back down.

'Exactly. Admittedly, the poster where she was portrayed as a semi-lion should have been a huge clue. The second labour was to kill the Hydra, a mythical creature with multiple heads. When you cut off one head, two grow back in its place.'

'Irina Oprea!' said Vlad.

'Yes! And then there are the Augean Stables,' continued Gigi.

'There's nothing there though...'

'Yes, there is. Two weeks ago there was a flooding at an equestrian centre in Râşnov. No victims, but the guard there nearly drowned. A hydrant burst and there was water everywhere. In the myth, Hercules changes the course of a river to wash those stables that hadn't been cleaned in thirty years.'

'How did you know about the flooding?' asked Vlad.

'Stop interrupting. I know because Radu was called there. A mare went into labour the next day. Total coincidence. Now, pay attention, please. Another labour had to do with the Stymphalian Birds – a flock of birds with metal beaks. So that's the explosion at the gallery. Stop, I won't take any questions at this time, because there's more. Then there's the killing of Hyppolite, the Amazon queen. That's Claudia Moraru. The Amazons had their right breasts cut off, so that they could use the bow and arrow with more strength and precision. That's what helped me make the connection. And there's one more. The Hind of I-don't-know-where. Do you remember the guy who complained that someone pushed him off the mountain in Postăvaru?'

'That's too much, Gigi!' protested Matei.

'Try and understand. It's all very plausible.'

'No, Gigi, it's far-fetched. What if your hypothesis is wrong?' Vlad agreed with Matei.

'And what if it's right? It's the only pattern that makes any sense.'

'But what if you are the only one who can spot this apparent pattern? What if we waste our time going back over the cases and seeing them from this new angle, instead of treating them as separate instances?' Matei complained.

'How about we try to work in parallel? On the one hand, continue treating each case independently and dig further. On the other hand, let's attempt to check out this overarching pattern. I might have something else too. OK, this one might be stretching things a bit. But I can't help wondering... what road was the building site where that guy was found in Bucharest?'

'Căluşei.'

'There you go! Căluşei, that means little horses! One of Hercules' labours was to tame the Horses of Diomedes – some wild mares I believe, who ate human flesh.' Gigi was all smiles.

'Oh, honestly, that's taking things too far! You can make a pattern out of anything! This is not good.' Vlad stood up and shook his head.

'Fine, you take the version where each case is independent, while Matei and I work on the connected cases angle. What do you say?'

'I actually think you might have a point there, but surely not the Bucharest case,' Matei tried to take her side.

'We have a bigger problem though. There are just six cases we've discovered, but there are twelve labours in total. Twice as many. So either we haven't found out about the others yet, to add to the chain. As you can see, not all of them are proper crimes. Or else there's more to come. If you're OK with it, I'll prepare a presentation about the Twelve Labours and how they relate to our cases for our upcoming meeting.'

'So you're going to create a profile of this new Hercules, right? Do you expect to finish by three this afternoon?'

'I'll do my best.'

'OK, let's give it a go,' Vlad finally chimed in. 'Put everything together on a single panel, or else do a Powerpoint. I want it to be very clear what sort of person we are looking for, because that's the important bit. I'll head off to my office now and try to think what to say to the press and when. I'll let Bucharest know we might have a new lead.'

'I'll get cracking on it then.'

''And what should I do?' asked Matei.

'Take these boards and bring them to the big meeting room and then call everyone in for the three o'clock meeting, even the staff out in the field, if possible. And can I use your office, please?'

'Sure. Log into my computer if you need, it's connected to the printer there.'

'No need to print anything, I'll prepare some slides. And can someone please get me something to eat? I'm starving!'

'I'll order some takeaways. Any preference?'

'We might as well do the whole police cliché thing: burger with fries and Coke, please!'

**

Gigi was smiling as she worked on her presentation. Things seemed to be falling into place at last. She refused to believe that all of these facts were mere coincidences. She did a more thorough internet search and listed all of the labours of Hercules in order. The Lion was Andrada, the Hydra was Irina Oprea. All good so far. The third was the deer or hind, perhaps the runner Cezar Condurache, who had been pushed on the mountain. The fourth was the Boar – nothing there yet. The fifth, the stables, must have been the flooding in Râşnov. The sixth were the birds, the metal sculptures and the explosion. Seventh was the Cretan bull – nothing there either. The eighth was the crime on the Little Horses street in Bucharest, despite Vlad's misgivings. The ninth was the Amazon queen, Claudia Moraru. That was all she had, the rest was mere speculation.

She barely noticed time flying by until Matei showed up with the food.

'It's two-thirty. Are you nearly ready?'

'I am indeed. Let's eat and go. Did you get anything for yourself?'

'Of course I did'' Matei dropped several bags onto the table.

'Will Vlad be joining us?'

'No, he's in his office, trying to sweet-talk the big bosses.'

'See, I told you he'd come in useful one day...'

'I have to admit I'm scared, Gigi. What if we are barking up the wrong tree?'

'Matei, I assure you there is a pattern there. OK, the one in Bucharest could be a coincidence, but I still have my suspicions. Any more details?'

'I've got some details about the victim here. He was a quiet guy, worked at a shop, Hornbach, had a family, yes, a bit of an alcoholic but with no history of violence. His blood alcohol level was off the charts when he swallowed the cyanide.'

'I think he picked him up off the road. Didn't know him at all. He was just unlucky, the poor bastard, it could have been anyone. The victim didn't matter at all, if my theory is correct.'

'Only you could come up with such a link between the cases! You must be as mental as this guy.'

'Don't flatter me.'

'What, you are proud of it?'

'Of course I am. We've got an explanation, opportunity and means, and I'm still working on a motive. I might have come up with one, you know.'

'Really?'

'Yes. I'll tell you at the meeting.'

'You're absolutely delighted with yourself, aren't you?'

'Yes, I am!'

**

The gentle background murmur grew more agitated as Gigi paused after presenting the first eight labours. She had a slide up with the four missing ones. She raised her voice to shush them:

'Please feel free to ask questions. About the cases, I mean. Try to overcome your initial response: that it's too far-fetched, that it can't be.'

'Could you please tell us about the next four?' Vlad asked.

'Yes, thank you. The order seems to be the same as in the Hercules myth. The two missing ones are the Boar and the Bull. They might already have taken place and we didn't find out about them. Or else he doesn't mind changing the order.'

'How do we find out which it is?' someone asked from the back of the room. The room was packed with all the teams working on the cases.

'I'm not sure. If we take into account the Bucharest connection, it seems the guy is being creative rather than literal in his interpretation of the labours. I don't know exactly how he interprets the boar myth for example, but according to the myth, Hercules captures the boar and takes him back to Eurystheus, who is too scared to accept it and sends the boar back. The Bull is likewise freed by Eurystheus, who incidentally is the guy who is setting all these tasks for Hercules.'

'So what sort of person are we looking for?' asked Matei. 'Have you come to any conclusions?'

'Hang on a second, let me talk about the other labours. There are three left, if the other two have already taken place. Firstly, we have Geryon's herd of cattle. Hercules goes after them, kills the two-headed dog guarding them first, then the herdsman and finally the owner, Geryon himself. Maybe we should extend our search to the surrounding villages.'

'Do you think there is a herd of cattle anywhere around here?' laughed Nicu, then turned the laughter into a cough.

'He won't take everything literally, but there must be a farm nearby. How should I know exactly what he thinks?'

'I thought you were lecturing us on the topic,' said Alina with some bitterness in her voice.

'Alina, I...' Gigi took a deep breath and counted to ten. 'I've got the main points of the story, but I don't know the details yet. It's just the most plausible connection.'

'And if we're wrong?' Marcel stood up, then sat down again, nervously.

'I understand your worries. But we have no other leads. Allow me to continue. The eleventh labour is stealing apples from the gardens of the Hesperides. Would he be content with merely going to an orchard and stealing some apples? I doubt it but I'm not sure. And the final one is capturing Cerberus, the dog who guards Hades, which is the underworld, the land of the dead. The dog keeps watch, so that none of the living enter that realm, and none of the dead leave it. Hercules doesn't kill anyone in this particular labour, just takes the dog back to Eurystheus, who once again is frightened by it.'

'So there's only one more serious crime to come? Involving a herd of cattle or a farm?' Matei raised his eyebrows.

'I can't bet my life on it, but it's possible.'

'Any conclusions about the type of person we are looking for?' asked Vlad.

'I've got a general portrait, and then a few particular traits. Bear in mind please that these are assumptions, but fairly plausible ones.' Gigi moved to the next slide, which featured a statue of Hercules. 'This is one of the best-known portrayals of Hercules, leaning on his club and wearing the hide of the lion he killed for the first labour. It's interesting that, although Andrada Vasiliu was undressed, he did not take the clothes with him, although the mythical Hercules took the lion's hide, knowing it would protect him in future. It acted as a sort of shield, nothing could penetrate it, so Hercules wore it in battle. Our killer only took a fingernail from the victim, but Hercules used the lion's claws to take the skin off, otherwise it would have been impossible to pierce. That's why he could only kill the lion by strangulation, just like the killer murdered Andrada.'

'So, to return to the general profile. In his thirties or forties, quite muscular and athletic, probably not too tall, not overly strong – the marks of his hands on the first victim confirm that. He must be quite well educated, probably university degree, to even know about all this Hercules business. OK, now this is where I get onto shakier ground, so hold on tight. I think he must have lost his family, his wife, perhaps a child.'

The noise in the room grew and covered Gigi's voice. She took a deep breath and spoke up.

'I say this, because the reason why Hercules is undertaking these labours in the first place is the fact that Hera, the wife of Zeus, his father, causes Hercules to temporarily lose his mind and kill his wife and children. He wants to know how to save himself, consults the Oracle and is told that he needs to serve Eurystheus for ten years and do whatever task his master gives him. I know this is a bit iffy. And very hard to check. But if we do have a suspect, we might be able to confirm that.'

'This is all very generic and vague,' said Vlad.

'This is all I can come up with for the time being. There might be some psychological trauma or mental illness involved. But I think this person is probably masking it very well. He must be quite functional. I'll work on it and figure out more of the details. I just wanted to share the big picture with you so that we can start working based on these assumptions. He became very creative after the first victim. That was the only case where he observed the myth closely, after that he started improvising. Hercules had a club, but the killer has never clubbed anyone to death. The lion's hide — the killer did not take any clothes, he might not even have kept the nail as a trophy. He certainly didn't keep any of Irina's hair.'

Finally, when she finished, Gigi collapsed into her chair. She saw Vlad getting up and giving instructions, but couldn't hear anything. She felt numb, ready to fall asleep almost. She shut her eyes tightly, then opened them wide several times. She remained seated while the others left the room. Vlad came up to her and put a hand on her shoulder.

'You're tired, right?'

'I'm exhausted. Can barely keep my eyes open.'

'Thank you, that was very good.'

'Thank you too. It feels nice to be appreciated.'

'By just anyone?'

'By you too, Vlad. Stop fishing.'

'Sorry, I was just joking. Would you like to go home?'

'I'm not sure. I feel there's no time to waste, but on the other hand, I'm not sure I can do any more work. What time is it?'

'Half four. Better go now and take a nap and then you can come back, if you wish.'

'You said I had to write a report for Bucharest?'

'Yes, but you can do that later.'

'Fine. Please take me home, and then get someone to pick me up again at six.'

'Six thirty. You need a good nap.'

**

It was the kind of day where everything seemed to be happening at once. Even the weather changed suddenly. The rain stopped and the clouds dispersed. When Nicu dropped her off outside her house, she almost felt like going for a little walk, but she could barely stand. It hadn't been a sustained effort, but an intense one, and this always exhausted her. She might seem all sure of herself from the outside, but the truth was it was always an effort. She could never shake off the fear that she would be found out. Usually, by the time she got to see the bodies, they had been drained of any semblance of life or of back story, they were mere puzzles to be solved. But today it had all been a little too close for comfort. The horrible way in which Claudia had been butchered made this the worst crime scene in her experience. It had never happened before. Never and ever were such big words to use. She felt like crying, but she never cried. There was that word again!

She took off her boots and noticed that there was hole in her sock, at the big toe. She hobbled round the house as if the hole hurt her. Morty raised his head to stare at her then settled back down on the sofa, ignoring her. She pulled the patio door open and stepped outside. She would have liked to sit outside, but the chairs were wet, so she remained standing. Her hands and cigarette were damp too, but she managed to light it nevertheless. She had been hoping to have a nap, but now she didn't feel sleepy anymore. She was afraid that if she closed her eyes, she would see the gaping wound in Claudia's neck.

She had always lived with fear in her heart. Sometimes this fear manifested itself as anger, which gave her the impetus to act. She remembered how her father would come home late at night, take one look at her mother and his lip would curl with disdain. Gigi was not aware of it at the time, but her mother must have been drinking. Her mother was pretty much constantly drunk. When she went to pick her up from the hospital lab, her mother must already have taken some alcohol on board, as her moods fluctuated, crashing like waves on the shore. She might hug her one minute, and whisper sweet words, then push her the next moment and say she was annoying. Yet, somehow, she had never been afraid of her mother, she could feel her weakness and there were still plenty of moments of laughter and tenderness. She would sometimes come to Gigi's bed at night and hug her, calling her 'my little one' or 'my golden Regina'.

She still felt guilty about not waking her mother up in time, no matter how much therapy she had gone through. Viorica, her mother, had taken a fistful of sleeping pills, she had plenty of them lying around the house. As a doctor, she could easily write prescriptions for herself, there was no computerised system for checking out the names back in those days. When Gigi had got home that afternoon, her mother was asleep, or so she thought. So she had warmed up her lunch by herself and then sat down to do her homework. But her mother must have taken the pills already.

She would never be able to overcome the feeling of loneliness which grabbed hold of her that day. That was why she was incapable of being in a committed relationship. Her father had woken her up that evening, said her mother didn't feel well and he was going to take her to hospital, but she had no idea it was anything serious. And then, when he came back alone the next morning, then she finally understood. Disdain and hatred can kill as much as anything, Gigi had discovered, but she had stopped short of poisoning her father. She finally realised there was nothing she could do to change the past. She had eventually forgiven him, maybe even learnt to love him a little.

It was too soon to forgive Vlad. Maybe she was waiting for him to apologise to her. Or was this an equally childish attitude?

She heard the phone ringing indoors, but it stopped before she could find it inside her bag. It was Lucian Conrad, missed call. While she pondered whether to call him back, the phone rang again.

'You are quite insistent...'

'Hello. I thought you might not have heard the phone. Was I right?'

'Yes. I'm at home. I'll have a quick rest and then head back to work.'

'When would you like to meet up? I'd like to invite you to dinner.'

'I just told you, Lucian, I can't, I'm going back to work soon.'

'It can be afterwards. No matter how late.'

'Lucian, please don't insist. I have no idea how long we'll be there. Things are getting complicated. A tricky case and I can't see you while it's ongoing. Please try to understand. I will get in touch once it's over.'

'Of course. I'm sorry you're so busy. I do understand, you know. May I still phone you from time to time?'

'You can try, but if I don't answer, then you'll know that I'm busy.'

'Sure. Or shall I let you call me when you have a spare moment?'

'That would be best. Good-bye, Lucian!'

'Bye-bye!'

She felt like throwing the phone. She was not sure why she found the man so annoying. He had been polite, if on the pushy side. Should she put the phone on silent? But no, what if the police needed to call her? Instead of going to the bedroom, she headed for the bathroom. She let the hot water run until the whole room steamed up. She slowly got undressed and stepped into the shower. The water was too hot, she had to adjust it quickly to avoid getting scalded. The heat was almost bearable now, and she got her hair wet too. It would take some time to dry it. Then she realised she was finding all sorts of excuses not to sleep.

She got into a pink woollen dress, looked for her grey boots and then put on a thick jumper that seemed to be twice her size. She stared at herself in the mirror, then felt too hot and took the jumper off. She looked for her phone.

Matei did not answer when she called, but as soon as she sat down in the armchair, he called back.

'Are you ready already?'

'I am. I was thinking of coming on foot, but it's started raining again, so please send someone to get me. Are you in a meeting?'

'I came out to speak to you. I'll send Nicu over. Did you get some sleep?'

'No, I couldn't. Or didn't want to.'

'Well, I'm glad you phoned me and not him.'

'I don't know what to say,' she said after a short pause.

''You don't have to say anything.'

'OK, tell them to give me a beep when the car is here and I'll come out.'

Even without that girl, Alina, she still wouldn't have liked to get too close to Matei. It would be too complicated. After all, being alone was her natural state of being. She felt safest on her own. She had always feared Vlad somehow. She had previously had the tendency to give in to him, afraid of incurring his disdain or his rejection. That old familiar fear. From her father, from Fora... She wasn't in love with Vlad any more, but she still felt that fear of rejection with him. But she had never felt this fear with Matei, maybe that's why she felt no frisson with him either.

Radu's number came up on her phone now. This was clearly the evening when all the chickens were coming home to roost.

'Hello, Radu.'

'Good evening. Are you at home?'

'For only another half hour or so. Why?'

'I'd like to pick up my remaining stuff.'

'What is there left?'

'A couple of things for my bike in the storeroom. My helmet as well. Can I come and get them?'

'Yes. I'll be out soon. And please drop the keys in the letterbox once you finish, OK?'

'Er, can I keep them? Just in case I've forgotten anything else.'

'Are you OK?'

'I... think so.'

'I am sorry, you know.'

'Gigi, is there any chance...?'

'Don't get upset, I don't want to make up with you. I just wanted you to know that I am sorry it didn't work out.'

'I did my best.'

'I know, Radu. So did I.'

'Well...'

'Seriously, I did, even though it didn't quite work out the way I wanted it to.'

'Fine, I don't think there's any point in discussing this further.'

'You're right. All the best, Radu!'

Cats are far more independent, that's what she liked about them. Morty jumped into her lap, headbutted her on the chin, then pushed against the phone in her hand. She put it down on the table and started stroking him. Humans resemble dogs more. They always need something, need attention, need to be seen, to be loved, and start to beg for it. Cats are far less needy, but if they want something, they are not afraid of letting you know at once. Without a care in the world about how you might respond.

18

The Ninth

Needless to say, it all went downhill once the schools started. The tourists stopped coming mid-week, it got busy only at the weekend. He had suggested to the owners that they should just open Friday to Sunday, or at most Thursday to Sunday, but no, they insisted on this idiocy of wasting the whole week but only really working three days. They paid minimum wage, because apparently the tips were supposed to be so great, but this place was never full, who the hell bothered to come here when they could go up to Poiana. As for the guided tours, the ones they liked to boast about so much, well, they seldom left a single leu, the tourist agency had paid in advance. If the guides had any sense, they would collect a small amount from each member of the group and then give it to the waiters as a tip. Or maybe they did gather the money but then kept it for themselves, who knows?

Unremitting rain all day, so of course they didn't have a single customer at the restaurant. If it continued like that, he would have to look around for another job. His colleagues had left the restaurant, he was the only waiter on his shift. At least they weren't all obliged to hang around and stare at each other like idiots. Just him and the security guard left. He went to get some leftovers from the English party who'd come at the weekend. They had been more eager to drink than eat.

'Here, doggy, doggy! Where is that mutt? I can hear him, but it's kinda dark outside. Come on, doggy! What are you up to?' he spoke out loud.

The dog was barking, agitated, running towards him and then back towards the road again. He peered into the dark but couldn't make out much. It could be that bear again, although they'd been told that they had managed to trap and release him further away. These wild critters had got a bit too used to human comforts, searching for food in rubbish bins instead of going out hunting. In his neighbourhood, on the outskirts of Braşov, the bears would venture out as far as the communal bins between the blocks of flats. Everyone would go out and stare at them, try to take pictures. They were close to the forest here, so there was always a risk of encountering a bear. But they regularly trapped them and released them back in the wild further away from the tourists, in Zărneşti.

He could see the dog's white fur, see him running up and down, then he heard a desperate howl. He hesitated, unsure if he wanted to go forward and see what had happened to the dog, or go back inside and at the very least pick up his phone to use its torch function. As he stood there, he felt a sudden pain in his chest. He fell to his knees, unable to tell what was happening to him. He raised a hand to his chest and felt something long and thin sticking out of it. He tried to pull it out, but lacked the strength. He tried calling Ionică, the guard, but his voice was fading fast. The rain fell in torrents over him, washing away the blood pumped out by his heart, where the arrow had lodged.

19

Matei was messing about with his phone, swearing under his breath every now and then. Vlad was standing next to the noticeboards, having rearranged each case. Gigi was leaning back in the armchair, not caring if her skirt rode up, contemplating the pictures from a distance. Nicu was still munching on his supper, alternating between pizza boxes. Paul had brought in his laptop and was typing something. Vlad finally broke the silence.

'So we're stuck?'

'Let Paul do his search, let him finish, be patient,' pleaded Gigi.

'He'll find hundreds of hits. The search is too vague, and we don't even know if we've got the right parameters.'

'Vlad, let him do it, this is our only lead,' said Matei, 'He's searching for women aged 30 to 50 who have died in Braşov in the past two years.'

'And Bucharest, please,' said Gigi, 'He seems to know that city well too. He is mostly active here, but since he has also killed there, we have to extend our search further afield.'

'Yes, but let's start with just here, OK?' Matei tried to convince her.

'Can we do it all at once, please?'

'Fine, fine as you wish. Don't look like that, Vlad, we've got to try it.'

Vlad muttered something and continued moving the pictures around.

'Stop fidgeting with those pictures! They're in the right order!' said Gigi, standing up.

'I want to leave a blank space where the missing labours are. Such as the Boar and the Bull.'

'There could be incidents that we never heard of, such as the flooding at the equestrian centre. If I hadn't known about it from Radu, we might never have made the link. But I understand what you're trying to do, it makes sense. Let's just put some information on there and see if anything appears that fits the criteria.'

'So we have cattle, a farm or maybe a sheep pen. Then, an orchard. And, finally, a dog.' Matei tried to help Vlad out. 'But where the hell should we look? There are plenty of farms and sheep pens all around Braşov.'

'Have you told the farmers and shepherds to be careful?' asked Gigi.

'No, we can't do that. People would panic. And we would look foolish. The press would have a field day,' said Vlad. 'It was bad enough that we told them that we are looking for a serial killer. They all jumped on us.'

'Did you tell them about the Hercules connection?'

'No, of course not. What do you take me for?'

'I'm sorry, I didn't mean to offend you,' Gigi put her hand on Vlad's arm. 'Yes, it's too early to talk about the labours of Hercules. I can hardly believe it myself. Although the pattern is compelling, there are times when I doubt myself and wonder if we are just connecting random incidents because we want to believe this theory so much. The guy who is doing this must be very committed, very convinced of the justice of his cause. It's all about him. And he's been increasing the frequency and intensity of the attacks, as if he were gaining more and more courage. I'm pretty sure he would like some public recognition, but we have to think carefully about the most suitable way to handle this. In any case, he won't stop until he's completed these labours.'

Paul gave a small cry of victory:

'OK, here are the results. And I warn you, they are not pretty. In the last two years in Brasov there have been 31 female victims between the ages of 30 and 39, 54 between 40 and 44, and 108 between the ages of 45 and 49. The figures are roughly five times higher in Bucharest. So, for example, if we are looking at those under the age of 45 only, there will be more than 500 cases to check out. Sorry, Gigi, I can see you're disappointed.'

'I was certainly not expecting such high numbers!'

'It's like searching for a needle in a haystack!' Vlad bent over Paul's shoulder to look at the results. 'Honestly, Gigi, we can't do this!'

'Calm down! It was just an idea, I wasn't sure where we were going with this, but we had nothing else.'

'We might have something now,' said Matei suddenly, 'Get dressed, we're going out to a crime scene!'

Everyone started calling out 'why' and 'what', so Matei explained. 'A waiter at the Little Shepherd's Hut restaurant in Poiana Mică has just been killed. This time our killer was more careful, he didn't get too close. He used a bow and arrow.'

'He's sticking to the myth again. Geryon was killed with an arrow that had been dunked in the Hydra's blood. But he's mixing and matching things. The shepherd and the dog were clubbed to death according to the myth, so ... But there's no way we could have put a guard on all the shepherds' huts and pens around here, and besides he went to a restaurant with that name, not a proper shepherd's hut at all.' Gigi looked down at her dress and high-heeled boots: she had picked the wrong day to get all dressed up. 'Matei, I'd like to come to Poiana Mică too, but I need to get changed.'

'Well you ve certainly been in and out, in and out, shake it all about today.'

'Stop teasing. I did good work when I was in, didn't I?'

'Fine, I'll get Nicu to drive you home and then follow us to Poiana Mică. We might be there for a while.'

She had forgotten the light in the hall on and nearly had a shock when she got home. She rapidly pulled on some thick fleece-lined trousers, a long-sleeved top over her short-sleeved one, a jumper and a purple winter jacket to match her trousers. It looked like she was about to go skiing, but she didn't care. She would rather stay warm – and they were bound to be hanging about outside for a while. This Hercules fellow was ratcheting things up, which meant that he was gaining in confidence and eager to accomplish his mission.

Just as she was about to leave the house, she saw the bowl of apples on the kitchen table. They all seemed to be rotting, with the exception of a lonely red Gala apple among the pile of Golden Delicious. She grabbed it and bit into it with unexpected hunger.

'I'm done, Nicu, let's go. I've never been to the Shepherd's Hut, you know?'

'I haven't either.'

'Will we find it?'

'Don't worry, I've spoken to my mates and they've given me the exact coordinates. I checked online and it's right on the road. A restaurant, nothing to do with shepherds, other than that the interior design is rustic, for the tourists. The waiters are dressed in folk costumes, might even occasionally put on a sheepskin.'

'How do you know all this, if you've never been to the place?'

'I looked at the pictures on their website and Facebook. But you know what I'm hoping for?'

'What?'

'To have something to eat there.'

Gigi laughed out loud: 'Really? That's what you're in the mood for? Didn't you have pizza just now?'

'Sure, but I've got a craving for some tripe soup, now

that I've seen you munching on that apple right next to me.'

'Sorry about that, but to be honest, it wasn't that great,' Gigi replied and showed him the apple she had only half eaten.

'What's wrong with it?'

'Nothing...'

Her mouth was full of bitter bile. That apple was very different from the others. She tried to remember when she had last shopped for apples, when she had filled up the fruit bowl, but she had been too caught up in her work and she couldn't remember. She decided to stop dithering, opened the window and threw the offending apple out.

'Why did you do that?'

'It had a bad taste. Come on, let's hurry!'

'I'm going as fast as I can.'

They only saw two cars coming down the mountain on their way to Poiana Mică. They turned right onto an even quieter side road. How many years had it been? Four, five even? Gigi had been working late and Vlad offered to drive her home. She had said she wanted to see some falling stars and they had ended up on this road, which had not been paved back then. They had stopped there, got out of the car and somehow ended up in each other's arms and her life had gone haywire. She stole a glance at Nicu, who was concentrating on the road. She kept wanting to call him a 'boy', although he wasn't as young as all that.

They finished the journey on foot. All the other cars had parked at a safe distance. One of them, a Jeep, had a light on the roof as well, so they could see the thin curtain of rain. The door to the restaurant was wide open and the body was less than two metres from it.

'Can I come any closer?' Gigi called out.

'I've taken everything we need, I hope,' said Matei, 'There are far too many footprints here anyway.'

She made her way slowly to the body, which had fallen

to one side. A black arrow was stuck into his chest, with something resembling an orange feather at its tail.

'I'll go to the autopsy, but my first impression is that he was struck in the heart. Is this a hunting arrow?'

Matei nodded, 'But hunting with bows and arrows is illegal in Romania. It's an arrow that has a special metal head – you'll see that when you open him up.'

'Why is it illegal?'

'Because it's cruel. You might not have such perfect aim and the animal could survive for a while with the arrow lodged in its body, before dying in agony somewhere far away. It's not just in Romania that it's illegal, but in most other countries as well.'

'So where did he get the bow and arrow?'

'Oh, you can buy them easily for archery clubs. You don't even need a permit.'

'So you can go to a shop and buy them without having to give your name and so on?'

'Exactly.'

'Have there been any other cases? Of murders with arrows?'

'Not as far as I know. But I've only examined the matter superficially so far. I don't know if reception is good enough up here for me to look into it further.'

'What about the dog?'

'He's behind the gate, on the left. The killer was less precise in his case, the arrow pierced his neck and he suffered.'

Gigi gently approached the dead creature. His eyes were still open and the raindrops looked like tears on his fur. Vlad came up to them.

'Hi. The killer only got as far as the gate, he didn't come inside. There are some deeper marks there, but it appears he covered his shoes with some kind of foil so as not to leave prints. He must have been waiting there for a while. And shot the arrow at the waiter when the guy came outside. He probably shot the dog first, and the poor thing retreated to die in the shadows.'

'Is there no one else around? No one heard anything?'

'Only the guard, but he was still on his way here. He usually stays overnight.'

'They must have CCTV cameras, right?'

'They do but the attacker must have known about them and avoided them. They're at the top of the restaurant and only cover as far as the gate.'

'They don't have any cameras overlooking the parking lot?'

'No.'

'So once again we have a big fat nothing, right?'

Vlad nodded and looked down in shame.

Emil approached Gigi, 'Hello, we meet in rather unfortunate circumstances here.'

'Hello, Emil my dear. I'd give you a hug, but I'm wet and, also, I don't want to contaminate the crime scene.'

'No worries. Awful cases we've been getting around here lately.'

'You can say that again. I'm dead tired. But I want to join you in the autopsy room tonight.'

'Thanks. I was going to suggest it too.'

Gigi looked around for Matei, but he didn't seem to be in the yard anymore, so she went into the restaurant. Everything was made of wood, smelling subtly of pine and rather less subtly of food. Sheepskins were draped on each chair. They looked cosy and warm, and she was frozen from the cold rain. A man in a navy blue suit was sitting at one of the tables, with a drink in front of him. The colour of water, but judging by the tiny amount in the long glass, it was probably ţuică, plum brandy. Matei was bending over to talk to him. Gigi waved at him: 'I'm off with Emil to do the autopsy. Who's that guy? The guard?'

'Yes, he's in shock. He found the body. The waiter was only 27 years old.'

'Any family?'

'A girlfriend who also worked here. We'll go and talk to her now.'

'I'll call you when I'm done, ok?'

'I'll come to the morgue later anyway, I want to take the arrow to ballistics. Now that we finally have a weapon, maybe we can find something.'

'That sounds reasonable. Give me at least an hour to process.'

'I'll call you when we're on our way, I don't think it will be very soon. Are you sure these cases are connected?'

'As sure as I can be. Whom are you sending to speak to the girlfriend?'

'Robert, perhaps Andrei too. Robert is gentle, he'll do well. Or so I hope. We haven't had such cases before, as you know.'

'I know. It's a terrible case. I wish I were mistaken. I see the whole team is here, chief inspectors, the great honcho from Bucharest and all.'

'No sleep until we are done.'

'I'm frightened, Matei. Because we only have two more opportunities to catch him, if my theory is correct.'

'You really think he'll stop once he has achieved his objective?'

'Yes, I believe so. We have to catch him before that.'

She got in the car with Emil.

'Are you the chauffeur too?'

'Well, there was no point in calling poor old Nea Pavel for this, was there?'

'Anybody still left at the Institute?'

'Only Istrate. I told him to stay put, because I wasn't sure if you could come and help, but he can go home now. How are you anyway? I feel like it's been ages since I last saw you!'

'I feel completely upset, I'll admit, with all that's happening. Have you seen Claudia Moraru?'

'The one with the slit throat? Yes, you asked me to handle the autopsy, remember?'

'Sorry. I'm getting all confused.'

'It was a horrible case.'

'I got too close to the murder scene, that's what it feels like. I'm furious.'

'That's the way you handle things, yes...'

She finally started to feel some warmth in the car and took off her thick ski jacket. 'Aren't you warm, Emil?'

'Not at all. I froze my butt out there tonight.'

'Winter is coming.' They laughed. The dark forest engulfed them on either side as they drove down the winding road. The headlights lurched from the trees on the left to the trees on the right, you could barely make out any shapes more than a couple of metres away. They shivered. Emil switched on the car radio.

The two-volume *Legends of Mount Olympus* by Alexandru Mitru had been one of her favourite books in her childhood. The first volume was about the gods, the second about the heroes. As a child, she greatly preferred the gods, she loved hearing about their temper tantrums and petty games of one-man-up-ship. It must have been nice, belonging to a polytheistic religion. More gods to pray to, and easier to accept the idea of sin when you saw what the gods were capable of. She wished now that she had spent more time reading up on the second volume, the Heroes. She should have remembered the Twelve Labours of Hercules better. She searched on her mobile for the next labour of Hercules, stealing the apples from the garden of the Hesperides. The garden was well-hidden and Hercules couldn't find it. The golden apples were very important – they belonged to Hera and were guarded by the dragon Ladon, a kind of giant serpent with a hundred heads, according to some accounts. She tried to imagine how the criminal might interpret this myth but realised that it was impossible to anticipate anything with any precision.

Once again she was struck by the sensation that the red apple at home had a particular significance. She felt nauseous, but decided not to mention anything. They would think she was going mad, seeing Hercules everywhere.

20

The Tenth

He fixed the headlamp around the top of his head once he had distanced himself two turns down the road, shortly before entering the forest. The rainfall was softer there, blocked by tree branches and foliage. He cleared the leaves to one side and started digging with his gloved hands. The earth was only moist on the surface, so he had to use his bow to dig deeper. Ten centimetres down was enough, he placed the bow and remaining arrows there, then covered them again with mud and dead leaves. He pressed them down a little, then returned to the Old Road. He could hear the police sirens somewhere in the distance. They had got there rather quickly. The guard must have called them, no thanks to that damn dog. He started running faster, but the shoe protectors made him slip. He stopped to take them off, they were of no use to him now, and put them in his pocket.

He checked the time. In twenty minutes he could reach Solomon's Rocks. It only took him a quarter of an hour to get there usually, but now it was dark and slippery. Without taking his gloves off, he readjusted his headlamp and increased the pace. When he got to the abandoned inn at the bottom of the road, he checked his watch again. Twenty-two minutes. His smile was concealed by the cagoule he had raised to cover his nose. He took off his headlamp; from here on, the light from the streetlamps would be more than adequate. He could keep up this pace until he got home.

He crossed Unirii Square quickly, throwing his shoe protectors into a rubbish bin. Then he turned onto a side street. Even if it took a bit longer, it was better than sticking to the main road and running the risk of meeting someone he knew. He loosened his cagoule and let it hang around his neck like a scarf. An ordinary jogger, nothing more. He made his way down Castle Street then accelerated at the intersection with the small street that joined the boulevard, stopping only for a traffic light. On Mureşenilor, there were only three cars waiting at the taxi rank, with five people queuing for them. Two of them were kissing under an umbrella, although it had stopped raining.

He could hear loud voices and music from the restaurant next to the County Library. He sat down on a bench. He needed to survey the place, he'd be back here before long.

He breathed deeply in and out a couple of times. He felt waves of happiness inundating his body. Everything would be over soon. He leaned back and idly contemplated the fireplace on the terrace of Kasho – the fire was burning even though there were no guests. A large group of people were coming out of the restaurant, he could hear their staccato voices, although he couldn't make out what they were saying. He heard laughter. They were heading towards the parking behind the library, but one of them left the group and came towards him. Should he wait a little longer? Come back another day? But what would be the point? If the opportunity so clearly presented itself, why should he not take advantage of it?

The syringe was in the breast pocket of his jacket. He took off the seal and held it tight in the palm of his right hand, with the thumb on the flange of the plunger. He stood up and approached the young man just as he was about level with the bench. The young man winced a little when he spotted him, but smiled back. He was staggering a little. He must have drunk a fair amount, so the effect would be immediate. He grasped him by the elbow and held him up.

'Hello, you had fun tonight, didn't you?'

'Erm, yes...'

'Got a light?'

'Somewhere, yes. Let me see...'

He plunged the syringe into his arm and pressed immediately. The boy took a step back, his face twisted in surprise and fear then he relaxed. He caught him just as he started sinking to the ground, and dragged him towards the path between trees. He placed him down in a sitting position. face leaning towards the tree trunk, then draped his arms and legs around the tree, as if he were attempting to hug it. He took a rope out of his pocket and tied the ankles and wrists together. Then he stepped back to contemplate his work, smiled in satisfaction. A job well done. He could go home now.

21

The empty pizza boxes were still on the table. Nicu opened them one by one, touched the slices that were left, then closed them again.

'What? Not in the mood?'

'No, they stink.'

'They must be stale by now. But I'm hungry too,' admitted Gigi. 'Is anyone going out for some food?'

'You mean, am *I* going out for some food?'

'Yes. I do mean that. Given that you're the only other person here.'

'Where should I go? What should I get?'

'Go to the Cafeteca at Patria. What's the time?'

'7:30.'

'Yes, they should be open by now. Get ten coffees, seven of them lattes, the other three double espressos. Get sugar separately. Plus croissants and any kind of pastries they might have. Here's some money.'

She handed him two 100 Leu notes.

'You want me to get stuff for all this money? OK, and where are they all? Are you going to wake them up?'

'Yes, get whatever you can find. Go, Nicu, and don't worry! I'll wake them up.'

The first person she called was Vlad, who did not sound fast asleep at all.

'Awake? I didn't wake you up?'

'Couldn't close an eye. This is the nastiest case I've ever

come across. Did you sleep?'

'In the armchair at the office. Everything hurts.'

'I can well believe that. Back at work?'

'Yes, please drum them all up. I'll go and wash my face.'

'You going home?'

'No, to the toilets here. I brought my toothbrush and hand towel.'

'Fine, I'll sound the wake-up call. Robert and Andrei are the ones coming from home, the others stayed here overnight.'

'Paul?'

'Has been searching for models of bows and arrows all night. He will have a list ready for us to check out. But there are lots of sellers of such stuff.'

'I know. But better than nothing.'

'Agreed. Coffee?'

'I sent Nicu out to get some, plus some pastries.'

'Shall we say in half an hour, in the big meeting room?'

'Yes.'

She was yawning fit to tear her jaws apart. She propped her palms against the wash basin in the toilets and looked into the mirror. Thirty-nine didn't sound so bad, but next year she would turn forty. She should have a birthday party – she hadn't had one since she was ten years old. Even that party had felt a bit forced. She had taken a few of her classmates out to McDonalds. Her father was only there to keep an eye on her mother. Her mother, when she had something to drink, suddenly became quite chatty, and she had played games with them, sang some songs even. She had a lovely voice. She would have liked to celebrate her birthday alone with her mother. She never sang at home.

Gigi tried to brush through the tangles in her hair. The rough cover of the office armchair filled her hair with static. She gathered her curls to the top of her head once more and fastened them with a hairclip.

She went down to the entrance hall and got herself a

coffee from the machine. Better than nothing, besides she wanted to smoke a cigarette outside. She pulled up her hood then heard Matei's voice:

'Hello, Fairy Godmother, how are you this morning?'

'Like shit, what do you expect?'

'Language!'

'Everything is so crap.'

'I didn't get to ask you last night, do you think the poor boy suffered? The waiter, Dumitru Ciobanu?'

'Really, his name was Ciobanu – as in "shepherd"?'

'Do you think that was deliberate?'

'No, that must have been a coincidence. Not an uncommon name around here. But I don't think he suffered. Unlike that poor dog who crawled behind the gate.'

'Now you see why hunting with bows and arrows is forbidden!'

'Absolutely. That poor young man didn't get a chance to utter a sound. The arrow went straight into his heart. I can't decide if this was precision targeting or pure dumb luck.'

'This used to be such a quiet town. It's gone mad now. People are scared. The media of course aren't helping. We need to issue a statement today.'

'People are afraid even when there is just a single crime, let alone a whole series of them. What on earth can you say?'

'Part of the truth. That there are several crimes that we believe have been committed by the same perpetrator. Something short. I don't want to list all the crimes, in case others cotton on to the fact that they resemble the Labours of Hercules.'

'I wouldn't mention the cases with no victims, or the one in Bucharest. Will there be a press conference?'

'Heavens, no. This isn't the right time for that. I'm sure they'll accept that we have work to do.'

'Will they? Anyway, here is Nicu with the coffees and food!'

Everyone was fidgeting in the meeting room, gathered around the table laden with food and drinks. They had only invited the people working directly on the case. Vlad Tomescu was sitting next to the projector. On the screen was a photo of the arrow they had extracted from Ciobanu's body.

'Good morning. Although it's, frankly, anything but good. Here is the arrow, and Paul has prepared a list of all the online and physical shops where you can buy these. Andrei and Robert, I would like you to divvy them up and check them all by this evening. I want to know who bought these and where.'

'What if he bought them from abroad?' Robert asked.

'Good question but unlikely. Hard to bring them into the country. Besides, it's easier to buy it in a physical shop, rather than online, where a credit card can be traced. Of course, it will take some time to check out all these shops, but hopefully that will have been his way of thinking.'

'Shall we check out archery clubs? I gather that he was very accurate, so he might have been practising,' said Marcel.

'You're right, you can check out the archery clubs. Although he could have practised in the forest, I suppose,' replied Vlad.

'Any prints on the arrow?' asked Andrei.

'You'd better forget you asked such a stupid question,' said Vlad, 'This person had shoe protectors to cover his tracks, and you think he'd have forgotten to put gloves on?'

The sound of Gigi's phone, set to vibrate only, was heard clearly in the silence that fell in the room. She stretched over the table to take it out of her handbag and switched it off.

'Sorry.'

'Do you want to add anything, Gigi?' asked Vlad.

'I'm not sure. We have the apples of the Hesperides and the dog Cerberus next. No idea if there will be actual victims.'

'We have the arrow. We'll see what bow takes that kind of arrows, there can't be that many models. And we know the model of a car that was seen heading down from the restaurant when the guard arrived.'

'Volkswagen Passat. Do you know how many of them there are?'

'Yes, Matei, I do realise that, but someone has to check it out,' Vlad raised his voice.

'Not sure if we have anyone left to do that. The others are checking out the deceased women over the past few years...'

'Give priority to the cars, that's more certain. And then check out the owners. Gigi, any further descriptions?'

She stood up.

'A man of above-average height, between 180 and 185 cm, to judge from the ballistics report on the arrow and the angle of penetration. Right-handed, so check only bows for right-handed people – which, admittedly, is the majority of them. He is of above-average intelligence, very calculated. Lives alone, with the stories he tells himself. He's probably a professional, in a job that allows for solitude, and a certain degree of autonomy. Age: between 35 and 45, athletic, fit, as I said. Not sure about his weight, but he seems very active. Somebody should also check out the cars that went the other way, up into Poiana. Any CCTV there?'

'Paul? Can you look up for a second and tell us?' Vlad raised his voice again.

'I was just checking that out. There is one general CCTV camera trained on the main parking lot in Poiana, then one towards the ski slopes. The Poiana Mică CCTV covers the parking only. But I doubt he went there, because the road to the restaurant turns off just before that. There is one residential tourist area, and two isolated houses, I will check those too.'

'That's about all we can do for now, so off to work, everyone!'

Gigi got up with some difficulty, keeping her head upright through sheer force of will. 'One other thing. The chloroform. I'm sure you can't find it just anywhere. Where did he get it?'

'I checked,' said Paul, putting up his hand, 'You can't find it in pharmacies. There is something on the internet but only for labs, and I believe it's not quite the right concentration.'

'That's what I meant. Medical chloroform is the only type that can make a person lose consciousness. The perpetrator has access to medical chloroform, so we should check out to see if any is missing from hospitals. Admittedly, he only used it in the first two cases and then again for Claudia Moraru. I think there was also the element of surprise for the first two victims, and he strangled them rapidly, but in the case of Moraru, I think he might have used an additional substance, so let me check again with Emil.'

'What do you mean?'

'He cut her head slowly, there was no blood spatter. Which means she must have been completely anaesthetised. So he might have injected an additional substance. She was full of needle marks, because she was undergoing medical treatment, so we didn't check carefully, but I will do so now.'

'So you think he might have medical knowledge?' Vlad insisted.

'Something like that. He either has access to medicines or works in the medical profession. Even as a vet, because they work with a lot of dangerous substances and are less carefully monitored. Or it could be someone who is very knowledgeable about chemistry. Doesn't have to be someone who works in the field, but a chemistry teacher, someone who has some connection to it.'

'I'll bear that in mind if we need to narrow our search. Once we figure out all the car owners and links to deceased women,' sighed Paul.

'How much time will you need?' asked Matei.

'No idea. But you know full well that the data is not aggregated, so it might take at least three days.'

Silence fell once more in the meeting room. On the table Gigi's phone started vibrating again.

A number she didn't know. At eight in the morning? Gigi went outside and called back:

'Good morning, I'm Gigi Alexa, you called me?'

'Yes, this is Flowers de Luxe. I have a bouquet for you. I was told to call you beforehand to check where exactly to deliver.'

'Who are they from?'

'It is our policy not to divulge that.'

'Yes, I know. Is there any message?'

'Yes. You will see it when you receive the flowers. Where shall I bring them?'

'I'd rather you read the message to me first.'

'I'm not allowed to do that.'

'But they are my flowers!'

'Yes, that's why I will deliver them to you.'

'OK, bring them to the police station.'

'Are you joking?'

'Do I sound like I am joking? I work at the police station on Titulescu. Please leave the bouquet at the main entrance and I will come and fetch it.'

'Of course. Thank you and I apologise if I've upset you.'

She was getting annoyed now. She tried to call Lucian Conrad but there was no reply, so she sent him a text:

'I assume the flowers are from you. They are still on their way, so I cannot thank you, but would like a confirmation.' She sent another text: 'This is Gigi. To remove any doubt.' She got a reply in less than a minute: 'Good morning, my dear. I ordered them yesterday, so pleased they will reach you early this morning. Wishing you a day as wonderful as yourself!'

Was that a smile in the corner of her mouth? Maybe.

**

Matei contemplated the hill outside the window, wrapped in a thick mantle of fog. This was the second night he had spent at the police headquarters. He put his towel under his arm, picked up his toiletries and headed for a shower. He had a set of clean shirts at the office, but he'd never had the presence of mind to bring in fresh underwear. So he would have to make do with yesterday's. Again. Maybe he could sneak home to get changed, but there was too much going on. There was no one in the locker room, so he got fully undressed. He examined his underwear carefully, without daring to sniff them. Then he decided to screw them up into a ball, entered one of the toilet cubicles and got some toilet paper to wrap them up in, and threw the whole thing in the rubbish bin. He would be better off without any, he thought.

He took the Gillette shaver with him in the shower and ran it over his head as well. It had become routine for him. He needed a mirror, however, for the finer details, so he got out of the shower, wrapped in his bath towel, and stopped before one of wash basins. There was still no one around, so he didn't bother to get dressed before shaving his chin. As he looked into the mirror, he thought that somewhere nearby there was another man probably doing much the same thing. A man who had used a bow and arrow last night. A man who was on a mission to kill, for a reason only he could understand. The thought that Gigi might be completely on the wrong track with this made him shiver. But the truth was, they had no better explanation, so it was worth trying.

The press release, however, was shit. Everyone would start moaning about police incompetence. Typical behaviour: when people are scared, they need to blame someone. Alina had sent it off and then had gone home to get some sleep. It was a good job that she hadn't moved in with him yet; this was the first major crisis they'd had at work since they got together, and she was not handling it particularly well. She accused him of still harbouring feelings for Gigi. Which struck him as such an idiotic thing to say that he couldn't even be bothered to contradict her. It was clear that Gigi still had feelings for Vlad. At least Vlad admitted it, he kept hassling her, while Gigi was pretending, even to herself, that she didn't care at all for the big boss. Vlad would have to work hard to impress her – but this tension between them, this need to impress each other, was doing wonders for the investigation. Meanwhile, he would have to talk to Alina and ask her to be patient and stop nagging him. As if she didn't know how stressful the job was.

He glanced once more in the mirror. He looked a good few years younger now, after shaving off those white hairs that had started sprouting on his cheeks. He pulled on his trousers: it wasn't very comfortable, but it would have to do. When he stepped out of the locker room with his fresh shirt on, he felt like a new man. He bumped into Vlad, who looked dusty and tired.

'Had a shower?'

'As you can see. Yes, I feel much better,' replied Matei.

'I don't have any shirts in the office. If the shopping centre were open, I'd go and buy one. But it's quite a trek to go back to the hotel...'

'Oh, you're staying at a hotel? I realise I never asked you where you're staying.'

'Yes, we sold the house when we moved to Bucharest. At first we kept saying we would spend the weekend here, but the truth is my wife is not keen on that at all. So now we are looking to buy something in Bucharest. We're still renting. But I don't want to move out to the sticks either...'

'The school runs would be a nightmare, I can imagine...'

'She would drive them to school, but my commute would be hellish, it's always busy on those roads.'

'So you're not thinking of moving back to Braşov?'

'It must have cost you something to ask me that directly. No, I don't think so. I don't want to do that. Of course, it doesn't depend on me alone, but I have the feeling things have calmed down at headquarters, so I'll just see this case through to the end and that's it.'

Matei was in no mood to continue the conversation. After all, Vlad's move to Bucharest had resulted in his own promotion. He was still not quite sure how he could have been so lucky. There were others, better connected, who knew the city better than he did. But the higher-ups had decided he was worth the gamble, and nobody dared to criticise their decision. Of course, they would always have an air of superiority towards him, consider him an incomer, a dumb Moldovan. That stereotype must have emerged when so many peasants from Moldova came to the city in the 1960 and 70s to become factory workers. They used to bring them in by the busloads, scouring the poorest regions in the north of Moldova to entice them with promises of urban delights. And it had proved beneficial for many of them: even the small studio flats they were given were a vast improvement on the rooms they had had to share with numerous siblings, back home.

Of course, Matei was different, he had come via Bucharest, where he had spent more years than he had so far in Braşov. If he were to get promoted further, he might have to head back to Bucharest again. But maybe he should settle down here there was plenty of work in this city too. Vlad had told him off for getting too involved in each case, that he should let his juniors handle cases themselves. And perhaps he was right – he was certainly trying to be less hands-on with the day-to-day cases. This case, however, was anything but run of the mill, he could not step to one side. After all, Vlad was fully involved in it as well. The heavy rainfall last night had destroyed most of the traces, but he could not forget the look of surprise on the young victim's face – it must have been a sharp stab of pain.

On the corridor he bumped into Gigi, who was carrying a bouquet of red roses.

'You've been out to buy some flowers?'

'No, I received them,' she smiled and did a pirouette in front of him.

'Who from?' His initial thought was that Vlad had gone out to the shopping centre for a shirt and brought a gift for her.

'You'll never guess...'

'Vlad?'

'No!' She burst out laughing, 'You're obsessed, mate!'

'Possibly. Radu, then?'

'Why wasn't he the first person you thought of?'

'I don't know. I have the feeling things are not going well between the two of you...' He noticed her face and stopped. 'Am I right?'

'Yes, we broke up. I told you, didn't I? The other day, as I was going out for a coffee...'

'Ah, yes. But when did you break up?'

'On my birthday. He didn't even wish me happy birthday.'

'Thank goodness I didn't forget to do that! But honestly, who are these flowers from?'

'A doctor I met at a conference.'

'Is it serious?'

'Who knows? I've only been out with him once.'

'Do you like him?'

'Hard to tell.'

'If you really liked him, the answer would be simple. So you don't like him enough...'

'Yes, there is something annoying about him. He's rather arrogant, rather patronising.'

Matei laughed and turned to go to his office. Gigi followed him.

'Are you coming to my office too?'

'Yes, I need to put the flowers in a vase here. I don't want to parade them all over the meeting room. If I may. We'll see each other later?'

'Not sure when. We each have our own things to check out. But if you want to use my office...'

'No, I'll be in the meeting room, examining the photos once again. And maybe there's a pastry or two left. Where's Vlad?'

'I saw him a short while ago, as I was coming out of the shower. He might have gone to pick up a shirt, he was quite upset that he didn't have something to change into.'

'I'll stay as I am. But could you turn up the heating, please?'

'Are you cold?'

'Why, did you think I was just making small talk? I know I have thick clothes on, but I would like to be able to take the woollen jumper off every now and then. I'm quite tired too, possibly.'

'I'll ask the facilities people. You might have caught a chill last night as well.'

Matei went to the window, where he could see the forest through streaks, as if the window were dirty. The rain was relentless and it was as dark as if it were dusk. A feeling of foreboding and anxiety gripped him. Braşov was once again headline news, with the usual scandal about police incompetence. Everyone was eager to shout and snap at them. Alina said that a cartoon of him had appeared in one of the online papers – a caricature of his large, shaved head and bushy eyebrows, hovering on the brink of the abyss. She told him not to bother reading the comments, they were just pointless and nasty. Freedom of speech meant the freedom to be as vile as possible, with no consequences. This was the second time he was directly attacked by the press and he didn't like it at all. In his adolescence, he would have beaten up the trolls, but now he had no choice but to ignore them.

He had felt a twinge of jealousy when he spotted Gigi with the rose bouquet. Yes, he had been in love with her once. She aroused his protective instincts somehow. He considered her vulnerable in many respects — but maybe that was just wishful thinking. And when she'd told him she had broken up with Radu, for just a brief moment he had told himself that now she was free. He slapped the top of his shaved head twice, a gesture he'd used in high school whenever he made a mistake in a test. He rubbed his eyes, which were really sore. He also felt his nose getting runny — maybe his clothes last night had been a bit inadequate. He should have put a woollen hat on, instead of trying to act cool.

He went to the meeting room. Gigi was sitting in front of the laptop, trying to finish her report. Every now and then she stopped to transcribe a recording from her phone.

'You do know there's such a thing as a speech to text programme, don't you?' he said.

'Yes, but it's so inaccurate that I prefer to type it up myself.'

'Why aren't you using your earphones? You usually wear them all day long.'

No reply, but she complied with his request. Nicu had started sketching on the panels under each of the labours of Hercules: a boar, a bull, a dog. He was now wondering what to draw next.

'Gigi, shall I draw an apple here for the orchard with the stolen apples?'

'The Garden of the Hesperides with the golden apples.'

'So if I draw an apple, that's OK?'

'What does it matter, Nicu? It's not as if this guy is

respecting the exact details, he just takes whatever he wants from each myth.'

'Do you think he has planned all of this in advance?'

'I suspect so, but I'm still struggling to understand what triggered it all.'

'Would you say he is mentally ill?'

'Look, we discussed this in Fora's case too. He clearly has some mental issues, but that does not make him mentally ill and therefore unable to answer for his crimes in a court of law.'

'You think there must have been a triggering factor for this?'

'Almost certainly. I have no idea what. The name of the street in Bucharest and the restaurant that was called Shepherd's Hut: all this demonstrates he is far more creative than I had expected. I wonder if maybe his wife isn't dead, maybe she just left him, or they are estranged. I'll call Emil and head off to the Institute, to run another toxicology check on Claudia Moraru. You can call to tell me when we are next meeting up for a full report – I'm sure there will be lots to feed back later today. Or so I hope.'

On the way to the Institute she changed her mind and passed by her house to change her clothes. When she got out of the shower, there were seven missed calls, three from Vlad and the rest from Matei. They were all within minutes of each other and she wasn't sure whom to call first, when she got a new call from Matei.

'What's so urgent?'

'Where are you? Are you ready?'

'For what?'

'I'll send Nicu to pick you up from home. I realised you must have gone there because I spoke to Emil who said you hadn't reached the Institute yet.'

'I was just getting changed, about to head out.'

'You're not going anywhere just yet, we have another case.'

'What? You mad?'

'Not me. There's a boy tied to a tree in Livada Poştei – the Post Office Orchard Street. It must be Hercules.'

'So he's been taking the metaphorical route again, the name of the place rather than an actual orchard.'

'Yes, like with the shepherd's hut. But this is far too soon. Possibly last night as well, as soon as he came down from Poiana.'

'Give me just five minutes and I'll be ready.'

'Nicu is on his way. We are already at the crime scene, taking pictures. Come here first and then you can accompany the body to the Institute.'

The rain had restarted with a vengeance and Gigi kept slipping as she made her way to the area which had been cordoned off. She could see the boy leaning against the tree, his head resting on his shoulder as if in deep slumber. She walked up to Matei while putting her gloves on and patted him gently on his back. The person in the white overalls turned round and she saw it was Vlad, not Matei.

'Oh, it's you, sorry.'

'Why sorry?'

'I thought it was Matei.'

'I enjoyed that warm touch.'

'Stop, Vlad...'

'Please, let's just run away for a couple of hours. I need to hold you in my arms.'

'I'll pretend I didn't hear that. We don't have time for such things now.'

There was a flash in his eyes which told her he had noticed that she hadn't turned him down completely. She was cross with herself, angry that she still felt a yearning to be enfolded in his arms. She turned to look at Emil, who was bent over the corpse. She squatted down to his level.

'Morning. Shall we cut him loose?'

'Yes, we're OK to do that now.'

They cut through the rope and laid the body out on a

plastic sheet.

'There's no sign of injury.'

'Were you expecting strangulation marks?'

'More like a blunt force trauma.'

'Why?'

'Well, you might remember I told you about the Hercules theory. I thought he might use a blunt object for once, rather like the club that Hercules liked to use.'

'I don't think he feels the need to stick too closely to the myths.'

'Obviously, given the present victim. This isn't exactly an apple orchard, is it?'

Gigi got up to search for Matei. Vlad came up to her: 'I know you're looking for Matei, but can you please stop avoiding me. I'll never do anything that you don't want to do yourself. I can feel it, Gigi, I know what you want.'

'I wanted to discuss something else and you're just constantly interrupting... Yes, what I wanted to say was that I suspect he wasn't planning to act again last night. He didn't come here prepared, maybe he was just planning to stake out the place. But then he got the opportunity...'

'Why do you think that?'

'He'd have brought an apple or three along, to sign himself more clearly.'

'We still managed to figure out it was him.'

'Yes, but he also wants to create a picture each time. He tied the victim to the tree because Ladon, the snake-dragon, was curled around the tree. So where is Matei?'

'He's gone to the restaurant to see if anyone heard or saw anything last night.'

'Who found him?'

'Some youngsters who had gone outside to smoke. They're terrified. Stuttering about smoking. I suspect they were smoking weed.'

'You're not going to give them grief about that, are you?'

'No. Robert spoke to them, threatened to charge them

with possession, but then promised to be indulgent. Anyway, they don't know much.'

'OK, I'll go to the autopsy. We'll talk later.'

'Good idea. I'll tell Matei as well, maybe we can go out together, all three.'

'No way. I just want to sleep. I meant, we'll talk later when this is over.'

'As you wish. Get some rest. Do you think this Cerberus thing will involve human victims?'

'I really don't know. I have the feeling he is speeding up. He's starting to get a taste for this, his decisions are made in haste. But I think we could all do with a good night's sleep.'

'OK. Best to have the next team meeting at eight tomorrow morning then. Plenty of time for you to write the autopsy report.'

'Fine. My regards to the others, bye!'

'Bye, babe.'

She hated to be called that and she knew that he knew it too. Before getting into the car, she took out her phone.'

'Hello, Lucian, it's Gigi.'

'Hello, I'm so glad you called.'

'What are you doing tonight?'

'Inviting you to dinner.'

'That's why I'm calling.'

'Well, you promised you'd call when you felt ready to accept my invitation.'

'Where shall we go?'

'How about Belvedere? I love the view of the town from there. Seven OK with you?'

'No, that's too early. More like eight. Or eight-thirty. I don't know when I'll finish here.'

'Sure. Do you mind meeting up there directly? I'll book a table for eight o'clock and wait for you there. Does that work for you?'

'It sounds perfect.'

Emil saw her smile as she got into the car.

'Looks like someone is very pleased with herself.'

'Yes, I am.'

'Want to share?'

'No, it has nothing to do with the case.'

'Fine then, back to work we go.'

Gigi was right. Claudia Moraru had been injected with a dose of hydromorphine atropine. Probably immediately after being stunned by the chloroform. Then she had been laid out on the bed and carved up.

Meanwhile, the young lad was just twenty-three. He had quite a high level of alcohol in his bloodstream. He had been out drinking with friends and was probably unsteady on his feet as he headed home. He lived just a little further on, on the road towards Poiana, and had taken a shortcut through the park. If he had stuck to the main road, he probably wouldn't have come across Hercules. Once again hydromorphine had been used, they found a needle mark on the left arm. It had been such a powerful dose that nobody could have saved him, even if they had found him sooner.

By the time Gigi typed all that up, she was the only person left in the office. It felt strange. She switched off her computer and took off her thick coat, which she had kept on all day. She had only just managed to warm up. She was starting to regret having accepted Lucian's invitation, but it was the only way to combat loneliness, to avoid falling into Vlad's arms once more. She needed some food, life, fun. She would go the restaurant, and if he accompanied her home, she would invite him in. And if he took the first step, she might take the next one.

22

The window was wide open, Matei smoking in front of it, when Vlad entered the room without knocking.

'I thought you'd left.'

'Have you read the report?'

'Yes, just finished it.'

'Have you got the same sense of failure that I have?'

'Yep, I have to admit it.'

'I'll go back to the hotel. Want to grab a bite with me?'

'If I'm honest, no.'

'Please. I hate being alone.'

Matei threw his cigarette out of the window without stubbing it out first.

'Don't you have an ashtray?'

'I don't usually smoke in here. In fact, I don't smoke at all while I'm working. But I've restarted, as you can see. Don't worry, it's wet concrete down below, nothing to catch fire.'

'I'd forgotten how much it rains here.'

'Let's not exaggerate. It's only been two days.'

'You know what I mean. Come join me for supper at the hotel.'

'OK, I will then. I'm not in the mood to see Alina anyway.'

'Have you had a fight?'

'She told me I've started to behave just like you, because I made her rewrite the press release three times this afternoon.'

Vlad laughed. 'Ah, so what you showed me was the final version? It wasn't bad. The whole situation sucks big time though. And it's not easy to live with someone who gives you orders.'

'That's pretty much what she told me too. Let's go then, there's nothing left to do here and maybe we'll get some better ideas tomorrow. Paul said he'd stay on until he gets some hits on his multiple searches.'

'He's really good, don't know what we'd do without him.'

'I don't know how he can keep going. He hasn't slept for the past two nights. He got Andrei, Robert and Nicu to stay with him they are shacked up in an office, smoking like chimneys. Anyway, their business. I told them that I need to have some clarity by tomorrow.'

The truth was that by the time Alina had showed him the third version of the press release, he had lost his temper. He had told her that she needed to give fewer details, yet hint that they had some information regarding the killer's identity. She accused him that he was trying to manipulate public opinion, then he yelled at her that she was calling him a liar. In the end, they came to a compromise: a few bland sentences, nothing that would set the world on fire or enlighten the public.

**

The restaurant was on the top floor of the Hotel Belvedere. Vlad went to his room quickly to get changed, while Matei got a table. To his great surprise, Matei spotted Gigi coming in. Had Vlad invited her along without telling him? Hadn't she said she was exhausted and needed to go home to sleep?

He was about to raise his hand to wave at her, when a dark-haired, elegant man in jeans and a black shirt stood up from his table and walked up to her. They kissed each other on the cheek. She was glowing. He led her to the corner table, the one with the best view over the city.

When Vlad came back to the table, Matei leant over to tell him the news: 'You'll never guess who's here this evening?'

'Who?'

'Look at me, don't turn around, because I don't want her to see us. It's Gigi with some guy, she's facing the other way. Don't turn, I said!'

'OK, I'll look later. Who is the guy?'

'No idea. He sent her flowers this morning – a bouquet of roses.'

'A secret admirer. So he's finally revealed his identity. She received another bouquet at the beginning of the month, and thought I might have sent it.'

'You too?'

'What do you mean?'

'She was so confused about the bouquet that she even asked me if I'd sent it.'

'Listen, Matei, I have to ask: are you still in love with her as well?'

'What do you mean: as well? Are you still in love?'

'I know we've never discussed this, and it's not the kind of thing men talk about, but I think we need to clear the air. I don't know how I feel about her. She annoys me most of the time, she's arrogant and intolerant, a complete smartarse. Maybe it's a matter of habit. I loved her so much once upon a time. And seeing her around these past few days... it brought back all those feelings I used to have for her. But Gigi is a strange person. Although, to be fair, there's something strange about all of us, that must be why we chose this profession.'

'OK, I'll admit that I cared for her for a while. Just after the two of you broke up. But we're really incompatible. She gives me a bit of an inferiority complex. Admittedly, that's my fault, not hers. A lot of people give me an inferiority complex, so I'm always on the defensive. Alina seems much more docile. I'm not sure if that's really the case, or if she pretends to be docile to appeal to me. Anyway, I almost feel a bit of nostalgia for the days when I was just having short romances on Tinder.'

'I know what you mean. I was doing quite well before I came back here. But don't worry, I'm not returning to Braşov. I'd rather accept a demotion than move back here. But so far it seems far more likely that I'll be moving to the Directorate for Investigating Organised Crime and Terrorism.'

'Really? They've made you an offer?'

'No, they merely hinted at it. But I have to wrap up this case first. If we don't solve it, you can imagine that there won't be any huge career prospects.'

The chef came to their table to greet them. He was part-owner of the restaurant, so his level of commitment was exceptionally high. He smiled and explained various items on the menu to them, then suggested that they should allow him to surprise them with his own tasting menu. The waiter brought an amuse bouche in a ladle-like spoon while they were waiting. He started pouring some wine: 'This is a rosé of Provence, Miraval.'

'Not for me, please.'

'Why, Matei? Come on, just a little glass. There are countries where it's perfectly legal to drive after just one glass.'

'I'm too tired and don't want to get into trouble. Look, there's a tiny drop here in the glass, just enough to say cheers.'

Vlad raised his glass: 'Indeed! Cheers to us, and may we find the murderer as soon as possible!'

Matei had to admit he was having a pleasant evening with Vlad, who finished off the bottle all by himself, yet still seemed perfectly capable of walking back to his room upright. Maybe it was easier for them to interact now that

Matei had been promoted, although he was still rather shy, but that wasn't Vlad's fault. He stopped to light a cigarette and smoked it in the car.

That was the second time in one day that he had gone against his principles. He had resolved to smoke only once in the morning while having his coffee on the balcony and then perhaps one in the evening when he got home. Not stink out his car.

Gigi seemed to have had a little too much to drink, she stumbled on the threshold as she came out. Matei nearly dropped his cigarette chuckling. The guy she'd dined with was holding her up, but there was something furtive about the way he was looking around and Matei didn't like it. Gigi was looking down, stepping very gingerly. She seemed to want to pull away from the man, but lost her balance, and he pulled her close again. They were heading towards the big parking lot next to the conference centre, so Matei got out of the car to see them better. When they got to the steps, Gigi tried again to keep her distance, but he put an arm around her waist and lifted her down the stairs. Matei took a step in their direction but hesitated, trying to remember if Gigi had told him anything about the guy. By now, he was virtually carrying her, and her head was hanging at a strange angle, all you could see was a golden mass of curls. Matei returned to his car and decided to follow them. The car heading out of the parking was a grey Volkswagen with Bucharest number plates.

He called the police reception. 'Can you please check a number plate for me. B657 HGB.'

'Just a moment. A Volkswagen Passat, registered in 2013, the owner is Lucian Conrad, living in Bucharest, Calea 13 September, number 89.'

'Thank you. Can you check his record, please?'

During the daytime, when there was a lot of traffic, it was far better to turn onto Mureşenilor rather than wait at the roundabout. But at this time of night, the roads were quite empty and he managed to stick close to the car he was following, although he did have to run an amber light to do so. He accelerated and was running parallel to the grey car. Gigi was barely visible, leaning her head heavily against the door.

'Nothing in his records, sir.'

'Fine. Thank you. Can you please arrange for possible back-up? I'm tailing a suspect.'

'Yes, sir. Understood, sir!'

All the 'sir-ing' was making him uncomfortable, but the poor lad was overcome at the thought of the big boss making requests. The car in front turned left on Agrişelor, which looked like he was taking Gigi home, but Matei continued to follow them. He didn't want to fall too far behind, just in case he was wrong and they weren't heading back to Gigi's house. He was telling himself that it was important to follow them, but in truth what he was doing was dubious. It was her evening off, after all. She could drink as much as she liked, meet whomever she liked. But something felt wrong about that guy. After all, she didn't know him very well either, so it was his duty, as a friend...

The man parked the car on the pavement just outside Gigi's house, got out of the car and headed to the passenger side. He bent over and picked her out of the passenger seat, she seemed to be fast asleep. He propped her up in a standing position, took out her handbag and started searching inside, probably for the keys. Then he hung the straps of her handbag from one shoulder, while lifting Gigi up like a sack of potatoes over the other shoulder.

Matei had pulled up a little further along and was watching these manoeuvres in his mirrors, but at that point he felt he had to intervene. He got out and ran towards the pair, just as Lucian Conrad was unlocking the gate.

'Good evening, I'm Matei Vălean, chief inspector of police.'

'Good evening,' replied Lucian, visibly irritated.

'Can I see an ID please? What are you doing with this woman?'

'How dare you...? I'll show you my ID after I have taken this lady indoors, put her to bed, you surely don't expect me to drop her onto the pavement right now, just to show you my papers?'

'Do you live here?' Matei was curious to see how the man would respond.

'No. She's my girlfriend, but she had a little too much to drink tonight,' Lucian continued, fiddling with the gate. 'If we step inside, I can show you my ID. But don't you think you should show me yours first?'

'Of course. Here you are!' And Matei took out his police badge. He bent over and looked at Gigi. 'Gigi, are you OK?'

'You know each other?'

'Yes, we are colleagues. One might say we know each other pretty well. Well enough for me to realise that I don't know who you are, which is something I don't like.'

'Ah, I see... Well, I hope you will know more about me in due course.' Lucian flashed a smile. 'I've only been out with her once before, for a coffee, maybe she told you about that, if you know each other that well?'

'Yes, she did. She met you at a coffee place near the police station?'

'So she did tell you, how flattering! You know, I really do care about her.'

Matei was speechless. He was beginning to feel very awkward.

'Would you mind helping me open up? I'm not familiar with the lock. I've never been here before.'

'So how did you know her address?'

'I checked her ID card. Thank you for the help. I can see you are very cross with me and I don't understand why.

Could it be that you are jealous?'

'How dare you insinuate...?'

'Don't get so het up! Have I said something wrong? Look, why don't I leave her with you to take inside?' Lucian put the long straps of the handbag around Matei's head. 'Please ask Gigi to call me when she wakes up. Tell her I'm not at all upset.' Lucian opened the door to the house and invited Matei to step inside. 'Good bye!' he said as he closed the door, his voice echoing faintly as he walked down the path and banged the gate shut.

Matei was left standing in the hallway, with Gigi in his arms. He realised she was quite heavy, which was a surprise, as he'd always considered her rather skinny. He placed her on the bed, but she was completely inert. He lifted up an arm and let it drop limply beside her. Then he lifted a leg and let it fall, heavily. She was too fast asleep. He bent over her but could barely feel her breath. He shook her and called her name, but there was no reaction. He was about to head to the car to contact the on-duty officer, but then realised he was parked some distance away. So he took out his mobile and called reception instead, getting through to the same novice PC he had spoken to earlier. He shouted at him to call an ambulance urgently and to do a callout for sightings of the car with the number plate had asked about it earlier. The young officer asked him to repeat the number. That's when Matei lost it and swore at him.

23

Matei's shaved head emerged from a sea of white.

'You're awake!'

'Where the hell am I?'

'At the hospital.'

'I can see that. What happened? Fora?'

'What Fora?'

'I was in the office and suddenly I felt sick...'

'Damn, Gigi, this seems worse than the doctors guessed...'

'Whaddya mean?'

'They warned me you might have a bit of amnesia when you woke up.'

'Where are we?'

'Don't start that all over again. At the hospital.'

'No, I mean... when?'

'Gigi, calm down a second and let me explain. It might seem a bit funny, but let's try to take things one by one. First, let's clarify the timeline. Can you be patient and listen?'

'Fine.'

'We closed the Fora case in 2018. We are now in September 2019. So let's put an end to the Fora chapter, shall we? I see that look on your face. Do you remember finishing that?'

'Yes. I was in hospital because I was poisoned.'

'That's right. This time we have another important case.

Does Hercules mean anything to you?'

'The Labours of Hercules?'

'Yes, exactly. So we've established the timeline.'

'But what am I doing here?'

'Do you remember everything about the case? What's the last murder you remember?'

She paused for a moment, then said hesitantly: 'The boy on Livada Poştei?'

'Perfect, so it's all back. Now, do you remember what you did last night?'

'Last night? We all had the evening off. Due back the next morning. I went to bed?'

'Not quite. You had dinner with Lucian Conrad.'

'The guy who sent me flowers?'

'Yes, yes,' Matei was out of his chair.

'No, please don't make such a noise, my head hurts. So what? I can't remember anything.'

'The bad news is that he drugged you. He put Rohypnol in your wine, that's why you can't remember anything.'

'Do you think he wanted to rape me? There really was no need. I remember thinking that if I went out for dinner with him and we had a good time, I might invite him back to my place anyway.'

'Gigi, I think it's more serious than that. What if he is Hercules?'

'How on earth did you deduce that?'

'He's a doctor and his car is the correct model.'

'And what? I'm supposed to be a dog? He was out to get Cerberus, remember? Don't look at me like that!'

'Maybe he thought he'd killed the wrong lion. Maybe he's going back to Square One. When did you meet this guy?'

'At the Urology Conference, on my first day back at work.'

'After the death of Andrada Vasiliu, right?'

'I think so, I'm not sure.'

'I can tell you for sure. I checked. Hello? Are you still there? Talk to me.'

'I'm tired.'

'OK, I'll let you sleep. Vlad will come to pay you a visit in about an hour.'

There was no reply. Gigi had fallen asleep.

When she woke up again, she remembered she was in hospital, and could recollect more or less the conversation she had had with Matei, but she still couldn't remember anything about the previous night. Nothing about the dinner. She'd forgotten to ask Matei how he managed to find her. With her eyes half-closed, she spied Vlad entering the room and trying to sit down without making any sound. He set down a large bouquet of roses, peonies and something else onto the bedside table.

'I am awake. Thank you for the flowers.'

'Good to see you!' He took her hand. 'I was so worried about you.'

'How did Matei find me? I forgot to ask.'

'You were so lucky! You had dinner at the Belvedere. That's where I'm staying and Matei came over to have dinner with me. He saw you in the parking lot afterwards and you didn't seem to be all right, so he followed you.'

'And at home?'

'Matei asked the guy you were with what he was doing with you and he got offended, hinted that you liked to drink a bit too much and then he left. We've put out a BOLO on him.'

'Matei said he might be Hercules?'

'It's a possibility. There are quite a few things that match the case. Do you remember what you discussed over dinner?'

'I don't remember a thing. I hope I'll recover my memory in due course, but so far the entire evening has been erased from my mind. The last thing I remember doing is sending you the report. I don't even know if I went home before dinner.'

'Matei said you hadn't switched the alarm on at your house. Why not?'

'Stupid question. How would that have helped? I haven't used it in a while. Anyway, I installed it because of you.'

'Can we bury the past at last? I'm sorry. There, I've said it. Is that what you wanted to hear?'

'Not like this, but it's a start. My wish to be able to discuss the past like two mature people is obviously not going to happen, so I'd better forget about it.'

'Indeed.'

'Do you know how long they intend to keep me here?'

'Not sure. Matei is the one who spoke to the doctors. But at least until tomorrow. Then I want you off the case.'

'Why?' Gigi sat up suddenly.

'You are too involved.'

'It was the same with the Fora case, wasn't it?'

'This is not the same. You're a victim now. Let us handle it.'

'We'll talk about it once I get out.'

'As you wish. Clearly, you have lots of things you want to talk to me about.'

'How I did NOT miss your jokes!'

She slept all day. They had pumped out her stomach, but she still had the sensation of wanting to sleep forever, she couldn't stay up for more than half an hour at a time. What time was it? It was dark outside. Where was her phone? It hadn't rung all day, maybe they'd been warned to leave her alone? She checked her bedside table, the drawer, but it wasn't there. Had they brought her in without her handbag, without her phone? They must have undressed her, she was in one of those horrible hospital gowns that tied up at the back. Just like in the movies.

She got up slowly and shuffled to the bathroom, still feeling quite dizzy. They had told her to ring the buzzer when she needed to get out of bed, but she felt reasonably stable. Why would they want to remove her from the case?

Was Vlad worried that she and Matei would accuse Lucian Conrad of all the crimes without any evidence? He would still be in trouble for drugging her – if he even admitted to that. No evidence, of course. The people at the restaurant would have washed out the glasses straight away. She leant on the windowsill. It was raining once again.

24

The first thing she asked Matei the next day when he came to pick her up was whether Morty was all right. When he told her he had fed the cat, she breathed a sigh of relief. Nothing else mattered. Once she got home to her living room, she sat in the armchair while Matei went to the kitchen to make her a coffee.

'Is the machine working? It wasn't before.'

'I can't hear you, but I'll be right back,' he said. 'Have you got any milk?'

'There should be some left.'

'Found it.' And Matei came in with two cups, which he set down on the coffee table.

'Let's have a party. Open the door to the veranda. I can't get up from the armchair. Tell me how you caught him.'

'We didn't have the slightest clue where he lived. He had given his Bucharest workplace address. So we waited for him outside the hospital yesterday. I wasn't expecting him to show up, to be honest. He didn't protest at all when we arrested him. He spent 24 hours in custody and then we had to release him. He didn't admit to anything, needless to say. The problem is we don't have any evidence. He said that you had been drinking and he had no idea why you got so horribly drunk after just two glasses. The prosecutor says there's no hard evidence that he was the one to slip the drug into your drink.'

'Does he have an alibi for the other cases?'

'Not really. He lives alone. I'm trying to find evidence to place him at each scene, but there's nothing conclusive. Very circumstantial indeed. I've brought you your laptop, by the way. What do you intend to do?'

'Read some reports. Maybe I missed something.'

'As you wish. As long as you stay quietly at home. We'll let you know if we uncover anything else. Are you going to be OK? Sitting here on your own?'

'Why shouldn't I be?'

'Maybe I'm exaggerating, but I'd like to send someone to stay with you.'

'You think he'll return?'

'If he's Hercules, he might. He's hunting you.'

'Hmmm... Let's not exaggerate. But anyway, do you know where my phone is?'

'I didn't take any of your belongings to the hospital. I left your handbag here. It's probably run out of battery by now.'

'OK, I'll search for it.'

'Here are your keys,' Matei put them on the table.

'I'll give you a spare set,' said Gigi, standing up. In the hallway there was a console with a set of keys. 'One is for the gate, one is for the door,' she explained.

'I know, I used them the night before. Do you still have the same alarm code?'

'Don't tell me you can still remember it? It's been ages!'

'Yes, it's 456478, isn't it?'

'How on earth...?'

'I remember being surprised that it had nothing to do with your birthday, so it stuck in my head.'

'You're fantastic. No, I haven't changed it, but I probably won't set the alarm.'

'Right, I'm off to see if I can place him at the scene of at least one of the crimes. Sticking to procedures sucks. I fear he will slip through our fingers.'

'Thank you, Matei,' she said and gave him a hug. He

squeezed her tightly and sighed.

'You really scared me, you know!'

'I know.'

'OK, let's not get carried away and sentimental. I'm off. Find your phone and switch it on. We'll talk later.'

She spent the rest of the day cleaning. Others liked to employ a cleaner to help, but she hated any unnecessary contact with strangers in her house, so she did everything herself. She took off her bedsheets and put them in the wash, shook out the curtains, vacuumed the whole house. The magic mop proved its worth once more, her floors were gleaming. She let Morty sit on the windowsill, since he wasn't a fan of going out in the rain, otherwise she might have tackled the windows too. Anyway, it would be better to wait for a sunny day.

The phone had been found and charged, so she put on her Spotify playlist while doing all the housework. Then she sat down at her desk and reread all the reports. She switched on the voice recording as she skipped from one tab to another.

'AHA! Irina Oprea had recently had a hysterectomy. Check out the dates when she was in the hospital, see if there is any overlap with Claudia Moraru.'

That was the only new thing she could think of. She went to the bedroom to put fresh bedsheets on. Morty jumped on the bed and tried to play with her.

'Come on, let me get on with this!'

The cat snuggled up to her when she laid down on the bed. She adjusted her pillows and picked up her book *The Secret Life of Corpses.* But she still felt restless, so she thought she might as well go through all her voice recordings once more, maybe she had recorded some bright ideas earlier and she could find a connection between them now. She found a long file, clicked on it and listened to a long recording, without moving at all. Then she called Matei.

'Hang on, Gigi, I don't understand. Please speak slowly and clearly.'

'I was going through my phone. You know I like to record myself whenever I get an idea.'

'Yes, you're quite annoying with your earbuds in all the time.'

'Well, I found something from that evening. I'll send you the file via email, but I think you can arrest him.'

'Who, Dr Conrad?'

'Yes, he admits he is Hercules.'

'How did you come up with the idea of recording him? Does that happen with just anyone?'

'No! I have a shortcut, if I press the earbuds and say AHA to Siri, it starts recording automatically. He said something about the actress and I started recording.'

'I can't believe it! OK, let me listen to it and I'll get back to you.'

**

Matei opened the file. The two voices were somewhat unclear, but that could be cleaned up by a specialist.

'Do you always keep those earbuds in?'

Matei heard the voice of a man – presumably Lucian Conrad. There was a piano in the background and a hum of voices. So even that man had been annoyed by Gigi's habit.

'Sorry, I'll take them off.' The sound was more muffled now, so Matei turned up the volume, but the background sounds got louder as well. 'You're right, I've had other complaints about this before. OK, I've put them away. So you were saying you were wrong about Andrada Vasiliu.'

'Yes, I thought she was my lioness, but it turns out you are.'

'Is that a threat?'

'No. An observation, merely. Regina – what name could be more appropriate?'

'Why are you doing this?'

'My mission.'

'Your mission?'

'I have to pay for what I've done.'

'What you've done?'

'Do you know you're annoying when you keep repeating everything I say?'

'I could get up and leave at any point.'

'Or you might not be able to. Anyway, tell me how you would like things to end tonight. Our meeting won't last that long.'

'I want to know why you did it?'

'I don't know what you are referring to. Perhaps what I did to you? I told you, I need to make up for my mistake.'

'Not me. Everything.'

'It took me a long time to recover after the death of my wife. It was a stupid accident. I fell asleep at the wheel. I woke up in hospital, not even a broken bone, but I'd killed them. Don't look at me with pity – it was my fault. So I had to atone for what I'd done.'

'By doing the Labours of Hercules?'

'I'm glad you noticed. Not that it wasn't obvious.'

'I have a question though.'

'With pleasure.'

'The boar and the Cretan bull. Did you just skip them?'

'Not at all. In a way, I was the boar. That's when I realised what my mission was. I moved to Brașov in 2018, to get away from that house in which I had too many memories. I went skiing and got caught in an avalanche. I managed to escape.'

'I see. And the Cretan bull?'

'What happens in Crete, stays in Crete.'

**

Vlad was startled when Matei burst into his office.

'I've sent all the evidence over to the prosecutor's office, including Gigi's recording. I think we've got him.'

'You mean the evidence we don't have. Do you think we can get a warrant purely based on the recording?'

'Why not?'

'Did he ask for a lawyer when he was here?'

'No.'

'I don't think it will be that easy, Matei.'

**

It was hard to explain to Gigi that they weren't able to get an arrest warrant in spite of her recording. They went to Dr Lucian Conrad's home address in Braşov – which he had freely given them after they arrested him the first time – and found him there, which they weren't expecting. They asked for permission to search the apartment, which he easily granted. While they conducted the search, he stood in the doorway and watched them. Matei was hesitant about handcuffing him. When he took out the cuffs, Dr Conrad had said that it would be an abuse of function, that he was being more than cooperative and would go the police station as requested, plus he had allowed them to conduct a search. So Matei didn't use the cuffs.

The prosecutor completed the paperwork but told them that the case looked too thin. Lucian Conrad was very calm in court, said that the voice on the recording was indeed his, but it was just a joke. Admittedly, a rather bad, sinister joke, which he deeply regretted now. He had nothing to do with the case, it was all a set-up so that they could boast about getting their perpetrator at last. But clearly the police had shown the same incompetence in this case as in that of the kidnapped girls in Caracal. He patiently pointed out that 'reasonable doubt' had to be overcome with definitive evidence, which they didn't have. He even said that Gigi had been so drunk that she had given him details about the cases before the recording had even started.

'And you're going to let him go tomorrow? Matei!!'

'Don't shout at me. We can't do anything else.'

'I can't believe it! That man tried to kill me and he'll get off scot-free?'

'He said he found it amusing to say that he was Hercules because you were so obsessed about the cases and could talk about nothing else all evening. So that was the way he hoped to grab your attention. He says the criminal is still out there and we seized upon him as a suspect to save our reputation.'

'But you can hear on the recording that he threatened me!'

'He says he was joking because you didn't pay any attention to him, so he invented it all. Besides, we checked. He divorced two years ago, his wife and kids went abroad. I haven't been able to get hold of her yet.'

'So there was no car accident?'

'Nothing major. He did damage his car in 2018, round about the time he divorced.'

'So you don't think it's him?'

'I'm sure he drugged you. But we don't even have evidence of that. He maintains that you drugged yourself, that it was a set-up and arrangement between you and us the police, so that we could find a scapegoat.'

'There's something more,' Gigi said in a small voice. 'I didn't tell anyone at the time, but I kept thinking I was being followed during the last few weeks. And I was sent some clues...'

'Clues? Like what? Why didn't you say anything?'

'Because I'm an idiot. I thought I was losing it, going mad, getting paranoid. I thought no one would believe me. For example, there was a wine that was left on my doorstep. Dark Horses was the name of the label, just around the time of the thing at the equestrian centre. Radu brought it in and I thought it was his. Then there was a magpie badge, around about the time of the explosion in the gallery. And then he left an apple in my house, so he must have come into my house. And the apple was bitter. It might have been poisoned, I threw it away.'

'Well, we can dust your house for prints, but I doubt he would have been careless enough to leave any. Oh, Gigi, you should have said something...'

'I know that now. I'm so sorry. So is he free yet?'

'Not quite. The boys are trying to delay things, but the judge said we had to let him go this evening. Or else he could sue us.'

'You're letting him go out of fear of being sued?'

'We searched his house and the hospital. We didn't find anything, although admittedly, we didn't confiscate his computer or his phone. He even let us access his locker at the hospital. There was nothing there. The judge said if we have no further evidence, we have to let him go.'

'So you called to tell me that?'

'Yes. I wanted to warn you.'

'You think he'll come for me?'

'I'm not comfortable with leaving you on your own. You're not a dog, as you pointed out, but he might think of you as Cerberus, the gateway between the dead and the living, what with your job. Shall I get Nicu to come and stay with you? Actually, I probably have to come myself.'

'You?'

'Yes, because if I send Nicu it means I have to fill in paperwork.'

25

The Last One

The mission of Cerberus was to guard Hades, not so much from those who wanted to come in – they were welcome – but from those who might wish to get out.

He had been in Hades for a long time. He kept wandering in it, lost, everything burning and pressing against him. The earth was molten, the streets flowing with lava.

The snow was hot. That was how he felt it. The day had started well, so cold that you could hear the rocks cracking. He had been surprised to feel such a drop in temperature after those few timid spring days. It was clouding over, but he had managed to take the larger cable car to Kanzel. Then they had to stop it, because it got too windy.

He preferred taking a shortcut through the forest on the Lupului Run, carving the snow with his skis. When he got to a clearing, he heard a distant rumble. He stopped to try and understand what the sound was and where it was coming from. He didn't quite make it to the trees before he was buried under the avalanche. He came to his senses after a short while, in a white sort of darkness. He could move his right leg, or so he thought, but actually any movement was confined to his mind at that moment. The left leg was stuck underneath his body and he couldn't be sure if it was broken or not until he got out. He had his phone in the inner pocket of his ski jacket but was unable to reach it. His right arm was stretched in front of him and he could just about wiggle his fingers, but his left arm was pinned underneath him.

He started twisting, turning his head from one side to the other, trying to create some space for himself, as the air was getting more and more difficult to breathe in. That was when he finally accepted that his wife had died, for him, for all intents and purposes. So had the children.

He awoke in hospital the next day – someone had probably seen him go off-piste through the forest, and may have even followed him to tell him off. That's when he realised what he had to do. The boar on Mount Erymanthus was the Third Labour of Hercules – but he was not the boar, he was Hercules himself. He had eleven more tasks to undertake, to do penance for his sins. He chose the Way of the Hero, he chose to become Hercules, the greatest hero of antiquity, and he would complete his mission till the bitter end. An end that would be waiting for him too.

Megara and the children were no longer waiting for him in this world. He had to follow them to the other world, and for that he needed Cerberus to show him the way.

And now, after several weeks, he had succeeded! He had completed all twelve labours. The light coming from above was white, as white as the snow that had covered him during the avalanche. Everything had started with the white, burning snow and this is where it would end. The moon was half-full and making the frost sparkle. This was the light that would guide him, help him understand what he should do next. Everything was half-full, somewhere between light and shadow, neither hot nor cold, neither black nor white.

The three-headed dog came towards him. He called out to Cerberus and Cerberus barked at him. From here onwards they would move together as one, there was no turning back. The labours were finished, the mission was over. He would soon be reunited with Megara and the children, and there would be abundant joy. He stretched out his hand to give the dog the food pellets. He kept on stroking him even as his body contracted. After it stopped moving completely, he still waited beside him for a while. He had been a faithful guide, but now it was time to follow him.

26

Gigi knew she should feel relieved that it was all over, but a sense of discomfort still hung over her. She would have liked things to be more clear-cut.

She had woken up next to Matei on Sunday morning. Had she let him stay over because she was lonely? Was it really him she wanted? After constantly making fun of him for his awkwardness, his inferiority complex? She had accused Vlad of lack of imagination for resorting to the cliché of sleeping around with work colleagues, but hadn't she just done the same? It was probably just as well that the phone rang so early – another corpse. Two actually, a man and a dog.

Matei got dressed and left without even stopping for coffee. That spared them any embarrassing discussions. She wasn't sure what she could say. Maybe she should have said something when they were on the brink of falling into bed together, but now it was too late.

A short while later, Matei phoned and asked her to join them at the autopsy. It was Lucian Conrad. His body had been found on the side of the road, close to the municipal animal shelter, holding a white mongrel with black spots in his arms. Hărmanului Close was a dead-end road right at the edge of town, hardly anyone ever went there by accident. What association had he created between this place and the final labour of Hercules, other than the obvious dog – well, now they would never know.

They laid Lucian Conrad out on one table and the dog on the other. Just as she had expected, they found cyanide in both of them. He must have poisoned the dog and then himself. Hercules had fulfilled his mission and had followed Cerberus into hell.

Gigi insisted on doing an MRI scan of Lucian as well. She had an inkling there might be some additional information forthcoming. This showed that when he had been buried in the avalanche, he had suffered a cerebral hypoxia which must have caused personality changes and hallucinations, although it seemed likely he had suffered mood disorders before. Perhaps that was one of the reasons his wife had left him.

When they finally got hold of his ex-wife, she explained that they got divorced shortly after a car accident, in which the children had suffered some minor injuries, but nothing severe. They had not been wearing seatbelts in the back. Lucian was overcome with guilt and was terrified of losing them. They weren't allowed to leave the house without him, she had to report back on every single thing she did. It was too controlling, too much.

The divorce had been extremely painful, but then, once it became official, it all stopped. He never even came to visit them and did not object at all when they moved abroad. She had wanted to get as far from him as possible, but he made no effort to contact them afterwards. Mrs Conrad, who had gone back to her maiden name, Greavu, said that Lucian had suffered occasional bouts of depression before the accident, but nothing serious.

**

They had stayed up late the previous night to tie up the remaining loose ends. The Cretan police had been very cooperative, keen to solve the case of a runner who had been poisoned with cyanide during the marathon. They confirmed that Lucian Conrad had been registered for the race, and even sent over his hotel reservation.

They had been lucky to solve the case, but she had been the luckiest one of all. If she had gone to dinner somewhere else, if Matei hadn't stopped for a cigarette in the parking lot, if he hadn't decided to follow them despite his misgivings, the outcome might have been quite, quite different. Every time she thought of that night, she could feel a heavy lump bearing down on her chest.

When they were reunited at the police headquarters later that day, Matei and Gigi behaved cautiously, as if treading on eggshells. At some point, he filled up a glass of water for her and she thought she detected something in his eyes, some sort of gratitude, but it was merely a flicker and then gone.

It was Nicu who drove her home that night. She went straight to bed, didn't even bother with her ritual evening cigarette. She thought of sending Matei a text, but refrained from doing so. No need to become too sickly sweet. After all, it had been just a one-night stand for both of them.

The following day, they had to complete the final report and hold a press conference to say that they had solved the case. They had discovered that Conrad had access to the hospital files of both Irina Oprea and Claudia Moraru, which was how he had discovered that they were alone and vulnerable.

They should be celebrating the victory, patting themselves on the back, but they knew all too well that Hercules had always been one step ahead of them. He had accomplished all that he had intended. Although they had discovered who the perpetrator was, they were unable to stop him before he finished his mission. They might try to spin it as a victory, but they all knew it had been a failure. Too many people had suffered.

Gigi searched through her wardrobe for something to combat the fatigue and disillusionment. She found a blue dress with a full skirt nearly down to her heels. She would show them what a stage entrance meant. She wanted to have all eyes on her. She gathered up her hair at the top of her head with a metal clasp in the shape of a golden snake. Then she put her lipstick on and twirled in front of the mirror.

Cerberus was ready to face another day.